WWIII

WWIII

THE WRITING IS ON THE WALL

A NOVEL BY

PHILIP LIENERT

Tate Publishing & *Enterprises*

Published by Tate Publishing & Enterprises, LLC
127 E. Trade Center Terrace | Mustang, Oklahoma 73064 USA
1.888.361.9473 | www.tatepublishing.com

Tate Publishing is committed to excellence in the publishing industry. The company reflects the philosophy established by the founders, based on Psalm 68:11,
"The Lord gave the word and great was the company of those who published it."

Published in the United States of America

ISBN: 978-1-60462-236-2
1. Fiction: Political   2. Fiction: Action/Adventure
07.12.13

Table of Contents

Retired at Age 42;
Terrorism Begins

This day had been circled on the calendar for a long time—
August 26, 1996. Lieutenant Colonel Steve Van de Kamp
was retiring from the Air Force today. He had been looking
ahead to this day for several years with thoughts of excitement about what would lie ahead in the next phase of his
career and life, yet also with a little trepidation. The Air
Force was a great way of life and took care of its own, as its
mottos proclaim. Steve would no longer be a part of that
and would soon be on his own and looking for a job. For
now though, it was a day to celebrate a big milestone.

Steve had a lot to be proud of and thankful for. He grew
up in a good family and did well in school. He was a good
student-athlete before that term was used much. After high
school, he was accepted into the Air Force Academy in
Colorado Springs. That was a demanding and rugged four
years, but the kind of thing that gave tremendous satisfac-
tion when it had been completed. Graduates often looked
back and recalled all the challenges and obstacles they had
to overcome to complete the degree requirements. With that

in mind and the degree in hand, they felt like they could overcome any difficulty in life—a great feeling.

In addition to that, or maybe because of that, Steve's career in the Air Force had gone well. His degree was in electrical engineering, a field he enjoyed and was good at. He had worked at Air Force Bases that did contracting with civilian contractors in the development of new weapon systems such as aircraft, missiles, munitions, radar, and communications. Steve had gotten his promotions along the way and was a great program manager, the title used by someone who managed development of a new system.

During his Air Force career, Steve had met and married Anne in 1988. They had two sons—Jeff, who was now six, and Eric, just six months old. It struck Steve that he had an infant on his retirement day; he was not quite a typical retiree.

As Steve, his family, co-workers and some superiors gathered in a conference room for the retirement ceremony, Steve thought back on all this: the career, the family, his health, all the travel he had been able to enjoy, some financial success, the Masters degree he'd added to his resume, and more. Steve wondered if this was all because of luck, or good decisions by him, maybe both, or something else. Steve had led a practically perfect life. He was not boastful about this, but reflected on such thoughts with a feeling of gratitude. This was all on Steve's mind as the room came to order and the retirement ceremony began.

Colonel Rutter did a great job of encapsulating Steve's career when he addressed the group. "Steve has had a big impact on what the Air Force has done since he joined. In his assignments from coast to coast, he has worked on programs that push the state of the art. He helped develop ways to do things better, or do things the Air Force could not do at all previously. That's the formula that has made this country great for 220 years. Next year the Air Force will turn fifty, and Steve's been a part of it for over 40% of those years."

That was a rather daunting thought for Steve, since the Air Force had been formed well before he was born. The U.S. started changing quickly after World War II. Born in 1955, Steve was part of the baby boom generation; a generation that would go on to greatly change the nation. Steve was still thinking about these things when it was his turn to speak. He passed on some of these thoughts to the crowd as he said, "I'm a planner. I like to set goals and then work towards them. I see my life as divided into chunks of twenty years each. The first was of course my childhood. Then came my twenty years in the Air Force, which I'm grateful for and proud of. Now I stand here at the halfway point in life. Next comes a second career of probably twenty more years until the final retirement, and then that final period in retirement. Thank you for how you've helped me and made the last years here both productive and enjoyable, and good luck to you as you travel down your path."

And off Steve went—no, not into the wild blue yonder, but to the back of the room to shake hands. Steve's parents were present and they chatted. His dad asked Steve, "So, you actually start getting retirement pay right away?"

"Yes," Steve replied. "Can you believe that? A nice little going-away present. It means I can take some time off before starting that second career and enjoy life a little."

"How do they figure retirees deserve to get retirement pay at your age?"

Steve replied, "Well, it's just always been that way. I guess it's to make up for the fact that military members spend a career being moved to a new base every three or four years so we don't get to put down roots, and we always face the prospect of getting sent off to a war zone to get shot at, and then we face mandatory retirement at what is normally the beginning of our prime earning years. Honestly, I don't really want to retire, but I'm being forced to. I'm young and more experienced than ever, but now they don't want me and I have to go start over somewhere."

Some more handshakes, some more old stories and reminiscing, and then it was out the door and indeed into the wild blue yonder for Steve, Anne, Jeff and Eric. Their plan was to stay put in Colorado Springs where they had been stationed for the last two years. It was a town of the right size—not too big, not too small, good job market, good weather, and a scenic part of the country. Steve's favorite football team, the Broncos, was just up the road in Denver.

On that same day in a different part of the world, Osama bin Laden attended a terror summit in Tehran, the capital city of Iran. The gathering attracted terror leaders from various places and organizations throughout the world, including the Palestinian Islamic Jihad, the Egyptian Islamic Jihad, Hamas, al-Qaeda, and Hezbollah. Bin Laden had established al-Qaeda in 1988 and began cooperating with Iran and its terrorist group Hezbollah in 1992. He and his followers tried to obtain nuclear weapons in 1993. More recently, bin Laden was financing at least three terrorist training camps and had just moved his base from Sudan to Afghanistan. He was continuing to fund and organize terrorism around the world.

During this 1996 summit, bin Laden issued a document titled *Declaration of War on Americans Occupying the Country of the Two Holy Places*, a reference to American troops being in Saudi Arabia since the Persian Gulf War in 1991. He issued a warning for American troops to leave Saudi Arabia or face Islamic holy war. Bin Laden stated that he would be justified in killing four million Americans.

The bombing of the World Trade Center in 1993 had been masterminded by Ramzi Yousef and funded partly by bin Laden. It had nearly succeeded. Some of the leaders had been captured, but some were not. Their near success only strengthened their resolve to continue their terrorist tactics in further bombings against ships, buildings, embassies, and the like. Led by its leader Osama bin Laden, al-Qaeda would come to be known for its patience and thorough planning. They knew how they wanted to do things, and they were patient in waiting for the completion of all preparations before striking. They remained especially interested in bringing down the World Trade Center.

The terror summit had been another step towards that aim and more, and also continued the relationship between bin Laden and Iran. The summit resulted in the creation of a committee that would meet on a regular basis for the coordination, planning and execution of attacks against the United States and Israel.

Christmas rolled around quickly. The Van de Kamps had been invited to spend Christmas with Steve's brother and his family in Denver, not too far up the highway. On the way there, Steve popped in a John Denver tape. The song *Rocky Mountain High* sounded great and more appropriate than ever on that beautiful day:

> He was born in the summer of his 27th year
> Coming home to a place he'd never been before
> He left yesterday behind him, you might say he was born again
> You might say he found a key for every door

When he first came to the mountains his life
was far away
On the road and hanging by a song
But the strings already broken and he doesn't
really care
It keeps changing fast and it don't last for long

This musician had always been one of Steve's favorites. He had never figured out why *Rocky Mountain High* wasn't the official song of Colorado. The lyrics and tune were an unbeatable combination. The words of this song were both beautiful and meaningful. In a couple years, Steve would realize the words had even more impact than he knew then; two words especially.

It was early afternoon on Christmas Eve when the Van de Kamps arrived in Denver, at the house of Steve's brother and his wife. The two families were happy to see and greet each other. The day was spent catching everybody up on recent news.

For years these family get-togethers always led to Anne and Steve comparing notes on what they had heard from relatives after each day. Both looked forward to it; at least, Steve used to, but the last couple of years they had turned into complaint sessions by Anne. Unfortunately, this night would be another one of those. As they got ready for bed, Anne started off a conversation with, "Guess what she asked me?"

"What?" replied Steve.

"If we're going to have any more babies. Can you believe that?"

"Believe what?" Steve inquired. "What did you say?"

"Can you believe she asked is what I mean."

Steve saw it coming, or rather, that it had started. He

continued, while trying to calm Anne down. "What's wrong with asking about that? We just had a baby. They're just curious if we might have more or not. People wonder about such things. We're curious about others. What's wrong with asking? I would ask if I was wondering." Steve had thought about how to handle situations like this for awhile, but nothing seemed to work. This time was no exception.

"Isn't that private?" Anne shot back.

Again Steve tried to soothe her. "She just feels close enough to you to feel comfortable asking. Isn't that a good thing?"

"It's my business, not theirs."

Steve didn't know it at the time, but he handled such problems the wrong way time after time.

Later, as he lay in bed but not yet asleep, Steve thought back to a morning a couple days ago when he woke up before Anne. When Anne awoke half an hour later, her first words were, "I smell furniture polish. Have you been using furniture polish?"

"Yes, don't things look nice?" Steve asked.

"Why?" Anne replied angrily. "You know I hate the smell of that stuff."

Poor Steve. He couldn't remember how the conversation had gone after that. All he remembered was asking Anne why she ever bought furniture polish in the first place if she didn't like it.

Christmas morning arrived still sunny and warm. The day was a lot of fun for everybody, full of presents and lots of food, and the kids were as entertained as they had ever been.

The next morning, the Van de Kamps packed up the car to head home. Before long they were back in Colorado Springs. Steve wondered what kind of job he would get and when, and how long they would live there. Steve had not pressed himself to find a job right away after retirement and was enjoying the new house the couple had recently bought and the freedom from work. The peculiar thing was that Jeff, who was now adjusting to a new school while Mom and Dad and Eric stayed home every day, was the only one who had to go to "work," but he never complained. However, time would prove soon enough that Steve had something far larger than this non-problem with Jeff to worry about.

TROUBLE AT HOME AND ABROAD

Life seemed good for now, especially when spring arrived and the outdoors could really be appreciated and enjoyed. There were few places more beautiful than the mountains on a warm day. The sound of the birds and the smell of pine trees when the sun beats down on them was something to behold. Then in summer came the afternoon thunderstorms, which Steve always enjoyed watching. Steve and Anne did a good job of keeping the household running, which was easy when both parents were home and had a lot of free time, but they seldom did anything together. About all they seemed to have in common was traveling.

They took a trip that summer into the mountains of western Colorado. The western half of the state had many scenic, smaller roads at high altitude off the highways. At one point on such a road, Anne stopped the car to admire the scenery. Steve got out and walked fifty yards ahead to take a photo from a better vantage point. When he returned to the car, Anne was livid. "Why did you take the camera?" she shouted.

"I got a great shot of that mountain pass up ahead," he said. "Isn't it awesome?"

"I just saw a deer," she said. "I wanted to take a picture but you had the camera."

Steve knew he was at one of those points where it was time to say something to try to calm things down. "Sorry."

"You're always doing that," Anne said.

"Doing what?" Steve inquired.

"Doing what you want, thinking about yourself."

Steve had apologized, despite not doing much if anything wrong, but it didn't help. "I can't read your mind or predict the future. How was I supposed to know a deer would come walking along?"

Whatever Anne said after that didn't matter much. A photo of a deer that couldn't be taken that would have just sat in a drawer collecting dust anyway was suddenly the focal point of Anne's life, far more important than the marriage. Anne seemed to let endless little things like that come between her and Steve. The boys were often nearby, hearing all this, too. They seemed to always take it in stride though; maybe they were just used to it.

Perhaps it was time to get back to work, Steve thought to himself. Maybe the fact that Eric, Anne and he were home all day every day was a bit too much for them. *We get on each other's nerves*, Steve thought. He'd heard of that happening to newly-retired couples. *These problems weren't as bad back when I was working. It's been nearly a year now; I've had my break and had my "fun."*

Steve and Anne talked about this, and both agreed that Steve would start looking for a job. That seemed a given. The new topic was Anne's suggestion that they start some couples counseling. They had thought about it separately in the past, and now discussed it together for the first time. They agreed to try that, too.

They each felt some renewed enthusiasm about changes

they hoped would come after that conversation, but it didn't last long. The next couple of months did not go well. Steve had never had to look for a job. "The Air Force: A Great Way of Life" and "The Air Force Takes Care of its Own" were more than empty slogans. The Air Force really had taken care of Steve well. It provided him with a college education, and then gave him instant employment after that. He did not have to look for a job or assignment; it was given to him. Same thing went for all of his reassignments and new positions after that. Steve now faced the downside of never having worked in the civilian workplace. He was not experienced with networking, resume writing or interviewing. His resume was impressive, but did not include employment with any civilian company.

All this seemed to be catching up to Steve. He found some positions of interest around town and seemed qualified for them, but he could not get the jobs. The stress of the job hunting leading to nothing took its toll at home. The fights, the arguments and the blaming went on. Furthermore, the counseling may have helped some, but was not making a big difference.

There was some good news. It was now winter, and football playoff season. The Denver Broncos had made it to the Super Bowl and Steve and his family watched the game in Denver with their relatives. The Broncos won the game, and they celebrated the victory as a family.

Then came the drive home after the game. Anne complained about Steve wanting to stay too late. She hadn't said anything until then, so again, Steve wondered if was supposed to read her mind, why it mattered now, and whether they could really make this marriage what it had once been.

Winter gave way to spring and then summer. The calendar and seasons changed, but the atmosphere around the Van de Kamp's home didn't. Steve still hadn't been able to find a job. He was starting to seriously question his post-Air Force plan of taking time off work. Maybe getting a job immediately and moving to any city where he could find work would have been a better plan.

One day Jeff brought some papers home from school. Steve and Anne saw something among it all that was particularly heartbreaking. Jeff had been asked to fill in the blank to finish the sentence that began with "I have a dream..." What he had written in was very meaningful. He had completed the sentence by writing, "I have a dream...that my parents don't get divorced." Instead of dreaming about going to the moon or inventing a time machine or being president, his thoughts and dream concerned his parent's difficulties. This simple piece of paper could serve as a wake-up call for them, but would it?

On Friday morning, August 8, 1998, two men in a truck pulled up to the rear guard shack of the U.S. Embassy in Nairobi, Kenya, which was manned by a local Kenyan security force. The driver demanded the guard open the gate. The guard refused, so the driver hurled a grenade at him while the passenger started shooting a gun at the embassy building. Inside the embassy, people heard the explosion and got up to look out of their windows, bringing them even closer to what was about to occur. The truck filled with explosives crashed into the rear wall of the embassy and exploded. A small bank building behind the embassy collapsed. An emergency generator ruptured and spilled thousands of gallons of diesel fuel into the basement of the embassy, which ignited as smoke and fire engulfed the embassy. An adjacent sixty-story building was also severely damaged.

That same day, a similar explosion rocked the U.S. Embassy in adjacent Tanzania. The two bombings killed 224 people and injured thousands. The plotting and planning of these bombings started in Sudan back in 1993, five years earlier. The United States knew of bin Laden's involvement in the bombings as well as his conspiring to commit other acts of terrorism. A $5 million reward was offered for his capture.

It had also been reported in an Arabic newspaper that bid Laden had acquired nuclear weapons from former Soviet Union countries through a network of influential people.

One day, Anne asked Steve to watch the boys while she left the house for a couple of hours. Little did Steve know that Anne was meeting with a friend of hers to talk about leaving him.

A couple of weeks later, Steve felt the need to get away, so he planned a trip to visit his brother in Denver for an overnight. Anne said it might do them both some good as well, so off he went.

The talk with his older brother did Steve some good, along with just seeing some new faces and a change in scenery. Steve was driving back home the next day. It was April 20, 1999. He turned on the car radio and heard what seemed like a special news report. There had been a shooting of some sort in the Denver area. Steve started to listen intently. He soon heard a recap of a developing grim situation. Two high school students were in their school shooting the place up. It was at Columbine High School, a large school in a good suburb not far from where Steve was just then. He noticed two helicopters above him heading west toward the school, and just then he also noticed that the highway was nearly empty of cars.

Steve listened to what was being reported during the rest of his drive. When he got home, he figured he and Anne would want to watch the news on TV and talk about it. That never happened, though. He pulled into the garage only see Anne's car gone. He assumed that Anne and the kids were at the store or library. That was also incorrect. Steve walked into the house and found a note Anne had written to him:

> Dear Steve,
>
> The day we married was the happiest day of my life. From nearly the beginning of our marriage though, things have been darkened by our arguing. It has been a struggle for us. Sadly, I believe the time has come for us to give each other some space. We'll be taking a vacation with my parents in Boston. The boys and I will call often and we'll miss you. I hope that in time you will be able to forgive me for leaving in such a way. I'm doing what I think is best. We cannot wait to be together with you as a family. Relax and enjoy your time of quiet. I pray we'll be home soon.
>
> All my love,
> Anne, Jeff & Eric

Steve was blindsided. He knew there had been problems, but he did not see this coming. Steve read the letter about five times. It contained some positive things, but some negative things as well. He had a lot to think about, and he thought about little else the rest of the day, and the rest of the week.

Anne called him that evening from a hotel. She and the boys were all right. She just wanted to reassure Steve and see how he was. Steve did not try to talk her into returning; maybe he heard in her voice that it would be useless. He went to bed early, but had trouble sleeping that night, and the rest of the week.

Steve was now alone in a four-bedroom house that suddenly seemed big and lonely. Anne had taken the boys, the cats and guinea pigs too; if it breathed, she took it. All this came with no warning, no discussion, nothing.

Steve and Anne did have some nice phone chats the first week. Anne even said that Steve's reaction to what she had done exceeded her best expectations. He hadn't ordered her back, or threatened to come get her and bring her back. He could see she needed some time and space so he let her have it and offered nothing but positives.

A week later, the nearby Air Force Academy called and offered Steve a job—no interview required. Steve accepted the position. Things were looking up. He couldn't wait to tell Anne. *This could fix everything*, he thought. It would get him out of the house and they'd each have their space and some time apart. Steve called her and told her the good news. "Guess what? I'm going to start working full-time next week at the Academy."

"That's good," she replied, uncertain of what else to add.

"What do you see us doing now?" Steve asked.

"I'm not sure."

So Steve inquired further, "Are you ready to come home?"

"I don't know," Anne replied. "Jeff made a new friend and likes it here. I'd hate to pull him away right now. Let me think about it."

Steve didn't know it at the time, but that was as close as he would come to getting his family back together. The next few phone conversations went from lukewarm to bad to worse. Steve was trying to do and say all the right things to change her mind, but nothing was working. Steve wondered what more he could do; what hadn't he tried? *I try to defend myself,* he thought to himself, *and she says I'm not accepting blame like I should be. I accept blame, and it just reinforces her feeling that it's all my fault.* The Charlie Brown Syndrome—Steve couldn't do anything right. *She wants us to fail,* he thought, *and she's practically doing all she can to help that happen.*

Anne seemed to drift further away and harden her heart. Before long, she wasn't using Jeff as an excuse, but was saying that she liked her new independence. The more Steve tried to save the marriage, the more it seemed like Anne was uninterested, was not going to let that happen, and was impossible to please. She seemed bound and determined to end the marriage and move ahead on her own, but she never came out and said so.

This dragged on for months with Steve wondering if divorce or a reunion would be the next step. Anne continued to ask Steve to not come for a visit, so he obliged, though he hated being away from his boys.

Steve had thought of many things to apologize for, and he had done so. Maybe he hadn't done it enough, or maybe not well enough. He turned again to the immeasurable talents of John Denver and wrote a long letter to Anne with the following song lyrics included:

> Our friends ask all about you, I say you're doing fine
> And I expect to hear from you almost anytime
> But they all know I'm crying, I can't sleep at night
> They all know I'm dying down deep inside

I'm sorry if I took some things for granted
I'm sorry for the chains I put on you
But more than anything else, I'm sorry for myself
For living without you

The song is appropriately entitled *I'm Sorry*. He had written a beautiful letter with the verbal intimacy that women like. Steve poured his heart out in other letters too, something he had rarely done before. Astonishingly, Anne didn't care about this or any of the good she saw and heard in Steve; she didn't even respond.

Before long, the time had come for Anne to decide if she would return for Jeff to start school back in Colorado or stay and start him to school in Boston. The answer came knocking on Steve's door one day: divorce papers. Steve didn't know how long Anne's mind had been made up about this, but she did exactly the opposite of what he hoped for, and she never even told him.

Steve spent a month trying to talk Anne out of this, but again failed. It became time for him to accept that this divorce was going to happen and let it proceed. He didn't have to do much; Anne's attorney saw to it that the necessary steps started to occur.

On October 12, 2000, the news was full of the story of the USS Cole. The ship had docked in Yemen for a routine fuel stop. A small craft loaded with explosives approached and rammed the side of the Cole. An explosion occurred which ripped a 35-by-36-foot gash in the ship. The blast hit the galley where the crew was lined up for lunch. Seventeen sailors were killed and thirty nine others were injured. The attack was the deadliest against a U.S. Naval vessel since an Iraqi attack on the USS Stark on May 17, 1987.

The attack was organized and directed by Osama bin Laden's al-Qaeda terrorist organization. Reflecting the hatred he had in his heart, bin Laden rejoiced at this and said, "The pieces of the bodies of infidels were flying like dust particles. If you could have seen it with your own eyes, you would have been pleased. Your heart would have been filled with joy."

This attack had been more than two years in the making. Bin Laden did not allow an attack to take place unless there was virtual certainty of success, helped along by thorough planning. His resources, including massive financial gains from poppy fields that produced opium and heroin, were spent on operations like this as well as attacks that were to come. Another attack of far larger proportions was now well underway.

LIFE'S BIGGEST PRIZE—
THE MEANING OF LIFE

Steve's life was in turmoil. The shock of the divorce papers caused a lot of soul searching and adjusting. Steve had led a practically perfect life up until now. Now it suddenly seemed like he had no answers to the questions of life, like how to be happy and successful. Suddenly, much of his life had been ripped away—his wife, his marriage, his children, his future plans—and he could not get them back.

Luckily, two things happened to help Steve. More precisely, two people came along who helped Steve. After getting the new job at the Air Force Academy, Steve happened to spot somebody one day at lunch who looked familiar. Steve realized it was an old friend, Terry, whom Steve had worked with back in the 80's for several years when they were both stationed at Wright-Patterson AFB in Ohio. They hadn't seen each other in fifteen years since then. Little did Steve realize initially the impact this encounter would have on him.

The two had lunch together and got caught up on what each had been doing. Terry was still an active duty officer and had experienced one exciting job after another since Ohio. Back in Ohio in the 80's, Terry had become a Christian and wasn't afraid to let people know it. He often steered his conversations toward that topic.

In the 80's, Steve was perfectly happy with his religious place in life and didn't want to hear what Terry had to say. Steve grew up going to church every Sunday. However, this didn't mean Steve had a strong faith or had incorporated religious principles into his life. The divorce caused Steve to wonder about this topic. He knew that many people had a much stronger conviction about God than he had. In fact, Steve had wondered for years about whether God would ever mean a lot to him. He had concluded that it was going to take some big event in his life if this change was going to happen. He figured the death of his parents would be that event, but now some other event had come along that might be the catalyst.

During that lunch and many subsequent conversations to come, Steve listened intently as Terry patiently told Steve many things about his own conversion. Terry quoted the Bible often. Steve was hearing things he had never heard before and was learning much. Terry mentioned 2 Timothy 3:16 in the Bible which states, "All Scripture is God-breathed and is useful for teaching, rebuking, correcting and training in righteousness."

Things finally began to click with Steve. *All Scripture is God-breathed*, he thought to himself. "So it's not just some stuff that people wrote 2,000 years ago that may or may not be accurate. It says it's the inspired word of God, that it's true and should be believed. If I believe in God, and I always have, I need to believe this too," he told Terry.

Terry smiled. God was opening the door of understanding to his friend. "It also backed up that statement with hundreds of prophesies that came true to prove its divine origins," he added.

Steve's life was now coming into perspective. He had always thought the purpose of life was just to have fun. He knew that was not exactly profound, but it's the best he had come up with, and it's how most people live.

One night Steve went to a divorce recovery workshop. It sounded worth trying because Steve was still struggling with Anne, sadness and regret. There were some married couples there together. There was also a woman there who was alone. She was attractive. Everyone in the room probably noticed her, if not because of her looks, then because she spoke up a couple times about what was happening to her. She was in the middle of a painful divorce and her soon-to-be ex was trying to take her son away from her. She was in tears at least once as she spoke for the whole class to hear.

Steve thought about talking to her during the break, but she spent the whole break time intently talking to the class facilitators. When class resumed, she left with one facilitator to talk privately. Steve did not see her again that evening, but he would see her again down the road.

Steve's new job was in a new field; he was now a budget analyst. He was serving as a civil servant at the Air Force Academy where he had gone to college. Steve had never been a budget analyst, but thought he would try it to get his foot in the door and see how it went, and he needed a job. He was a "number cruncher." It was monotonous work with little to show for his time after eight hours at the office.

But one day at work, something did happen that cheered Steve up. He went to the other end of his building to meet someone he needed to work with on a budget problem. It was none other than the woman from the divorce workshop. Steve got excited, yet didn't know if she would even recognize him. He introduced himself, as did she. Her name was Mary. She was in a much better mood than that night at class. She didn't recognize Steve from the class, but was glad to meet him and seemed to want to make a friend, especially when Steve brought up the topic of the workshop.

Mary's husband had recently filed for a divorce that she did not want. She had previously been stationed at Wright–Patterson AFB, like Steve. Steve and Mary were both using the same marriage counselor. She had a son the same age as Eric. Her son and Eric had both been born at the same hospital. They practically looked like twins. It got pretty spooky as Steve and Mary discovered more similarities they had with each other.

Mary jumped at the chance to talk about things with someone with whom she had so much in common. Steve knew exactly what she meant. The biggest thought he had after the workshop was the comforting knowledge that he wasn't the only person in the world who was getting a divorce, not the only person who had screwed up a marriage, not the only one who was sad and full of regrets and wondering how to proceed. Mary was in the same boat.

Steve proceeded to see Mary fairly often at work. Sometimes they needed to talk for work, sometimes they just ran into each other, and sometimes Steve made sure he ran into her. After a few weeks, they started getting together away from work for dinner or a movie.

Steve hadn't gone out looking for love in someone new, but he had found it. He started falling for her the day they met. Mary was outgoing, friendly and talkative. She could tell a story as well as anyone. She had lots of stories and she was quite funny. She was also a caring person. Steve wondered if she was like this with everyone or felt special about him. She had personality and looks to match—the whole package. Steve loved seeing her, looking at her, and talking to her. He wondered why anybody would want to divorce her.

At the urging of his attorney, John, Steve was taking every class he could find on every applicable topic: relationships, conflict resolution, parenting, managing a divorce, you name it. Steve wondered why he hadn't take advantage of such resources before it was too late to save things with Anne. He knew however that he was growing and learning in many ways; ways that would enable him to make somebody a great husband some day. *Someday*, he thought, *somebody will benefit from this.*

Steve still got together with Terry often. Terry always knew what to say. Steve always felt conversations with Terry were like talking to a chaplain. Terry would have been great at that or been a great counselor. Steve's way of thinking about things continued to change. He heard a great sermon on the importance and power of forgiveness. He discovered the ease and need to verify what he heard by reading the Bible on a topic like forgiveness where it says:

> If you forgive men when they sin against you,
> your heavenly Father will also forgive you. But
> if you do not forgive men their sins, your Father
> will not forgive your sins.   *Matthew 6:14*

Steve was getting wisdom, the kind that God supplies, the kind that matters, the kind that's hard to get in this world. This made it easier to deal with Anne—not easy, but easier. Steve had never read a Bible, and seldom prayed or talked about God. Terry did all these things routinely. Terry talked often about how he had gotten nearly impossible Air Force assignments, such as with NASA one time, and in his home state of Hawaii another time. He credited God for all this, not luck or his own ability.

Steve came to realize that religion, which he got plenty of in his childhood and since, was useless unless it taught and preached that Jesus Christ died for us, and that placing our faith in Him was the one and only way to heaven.

"So, you're saying being a 'good person' sounds nice, but doesn't cut it?" he asked Terry.

Terry explained, "Being a good person means putting your faith in yourself, and that doesn't work since no one is good enough. It says so in many places. The clearest is probably Ephesians 2:8–9, which says it is by grace that you have been saved, through faith. It is the gift of God—not by works, so that no one can boast."

Steve was ready to take that big step and accept Jesus as his Savior, the basis of true Christianity. Terry was eager to help. It didn't take much, simply a prayer of faith in Jesus that is believed in the heart.

After the prayer, Steve remarked, "That seems too simple. Isn't more required?"

Terry had heard that before and responded, "No, that's it. It seems simple, but it's hard enough that many people live seventy, eighty, even ninety years but never do what you just did. Most religions cater to man's desire to do more. It's human instinct to want prove how good and deserving we are, to do it on our own. Most religions were started based upon just that—ignoring Jesus while making ourselves feel good and proud—but God loves a humble heart and hates a proud heart, as it says in Matthew 23:12. Congratulations, you're now born again!"

"Born again..." Steve rang out. "Just like in John Denver's lyrics."

Terry, a good singer and guitar player, said, "Yes, I know the song you mean, although I think his 'born again' was different. Jesus said three times in John chapter three that no one can see or enter the kingdom of God unless he is born again. Most people live their life but never know what it means, even if they read it or hear it at all."

Steve was baptized the following Sunday. He had been baptized as a baby, but wanted to do it now as an adult. When someone made that decision for him forty-five years ago, it seemed to him now to be meaningless. Now he made the decision for himself. He was now baptized as an adult, like every single person whose baptism was described in the Bible.

A different religious ritual was going on at that moment in a different part of the world. At a terrorist training camp in the mountains of Afghanistan, a cameraman was filming what he saw. Footage included Osama bin Laden as he walked among and greeted other men, some with masks and automatic weapons. He met with some of the other leaders of an upcoming operation. Everything from words of encouragement to detailed planning could be heard.

The video included a testimony from Mohammed Atta, and the last will and testaments of two other men who apparently didn't think they would be around much longer. The footage also showed scenes of training at the camp such as militants performing martial arts, kickboxing, learning how to break the hold of someone who grabbed them, and practicing hiding and pulling out knives.

Al Qaeda prepared such videos concerning each of their attacks, both before and after the attack, to memorialize each one. In fact, they produced videos like this for any significant event to raise morale and boost recruitment, to speak to their supporters, to facilitate fundraising, and for psychological warfare purposes as well.

In this particular tape, bin Laden proclaimed he was confident that victory would be achieved, and he called on all jihadists to unite on the battlefield.

One Saturday morning that summer, Steve heard a knock on the door. He answered it to find Mary there. She invited Steve to go with her and her son up to the big water park in Denver for the day.

Off they went to Denver on a beautiful day. The three of them had a great time there, as Steve usually did when Mary was around. The only thing more fun than the water park for Steve was Mary's friendship and presence.

On the way back home, Steve decided to say to her what he had wanted to say for quite some time. He looked at Mary and asked, "Do you get the feeling we were meant to be more than friends?"

Mary took a second and then said, "No...I think we were just meant to meet, be friends, and help each other. We've done that, and I'm glad." She assumed this was not what Steve wanted to hear, and she hoped he would take it well.

He did. He had hoped for a different answer, but rather expected the answer he got. It didn't really bother him or ruin his day at all.

In fact, the day was not over. They arrived back at Steve's house, which had lots of great little boy toys that her son loved to play with. He invited them in, and Mary wanted very much to talk some more so she accepted. They wound up in Eric's bedroom, the room with the best toys. The room and toys had sat there empty and untouched since Eric left with Anne and Jeff, which was now over a year ago. Mary read a couple books to her son. Once again, her storytelling skills shone through. Steve watched and listened, and daydreamed. *How awesome it would be to be married to her*, he thought, *to do things like this with her every day*.

It was a day Steve would never forget. He was officially crazy about Mary. He thought about her all the time. He was still married to Anne, despite not having seen her for over a year. Part of Steve still loved Anne also. He would continue to patiently hope that either Anne or Mary would change her mind.

The next day Steve went over to Terry's house where he had been invited for a cookout. He was still on a high from the previous day. That would last all day, until the news he got later that day. Terry told Steve that he had a disease. He had found out about it just a couple of weeks ago. It was serious, one of those Lou Gehrig-type of diseases that doctors don't know how anyone catches, and worse, they can't treat it. He had been told that his lungs were going to fill with scar tissue from the bottom up, and eventually he would be unable to breathe—and it was terminal. This had already been going on now for over a month.

"Isn't there something they can do?" Steve asked.

Terry said, "They could do a double lung transplant that might work. I've read about it and thought about it. It's risky and life would never the same even if it does work. I don't want that. It's just too much."

Steve felt terrible. They talked for a while longer and then they hugged good-bye. On the way home, Steve reflected on how well Terry seemed to handle this.

He saw and heard more of the same from Terry as the next couple of weeks went by. Steve made a point of calling and visiting him more often.

Two weeks later, Terry died. Steve found this out from Terry's wife, whom Steve had come to know fairly well during the last several months. Steve didn't know what to say to her. Her loss was much greater than Steve's, but yet he felt that she seemed to be prepared for this and accepted it, despite the relative speed with which it had happened.

At the funeral a few days later, Steve found out he was right about that. The funeral was very well attended by Terry's many relatives and friends. Obviously Terry had been someone who had been outgoing, helpful and generous with his time with far more than just Steve. Steve listened to some eulogies. His wife even spoke. The common theme was Terry's faith.

Words were spoken about how God makes provisions and plans for each of us. We have free will which leads many to go off on their own, but to those who look for and follow the plan, God's plan is great. Even now at the moment of early death, God's plan cannot be questioned. This death seemed like a tragic mistake, but through the lens of God's plan for the world and mankind, things happen that we do not begin to understand, at least not during our lifetimes. That is said so well in 1 Corinthians 13:12:

> "Now we see but a poor reflection as in a mirror;
> then we shall see face to face. Now I know in
> part; then I shall know fully."

Terry's wife read this to the gathering that day and shared her faith. It was this power that got her through this sad day and recent weeks. She even told a story that day. "How do we explain it when something like a car accident or disease takes a life? Well, there was the shooting of 13 students at the school in Denver last year. Afterwards the story came out of one girl with a gun to her head who was asked by the killer if she believes in God. She said yes, and then he shot her and killed her. I've often imagined God welcoming her into heaven and saying, 'Daughter, you did something extraordinary for me.' I can barely imagine how proud He was of her, and what rewards lay ahead for her, not because of her act, but because of her faith. Here we are still talking about her and learning from her. That's God's plan." Steve was now almost in tears for the first time that day.

She knew that Terry was now in heaven and that she would see him again some day. She didn't assume this like most people do; she knew it. Previous funerals Steve attended had been much sadder. Steve now realized that was because most people just think or hope or assume they will get to heaven, but they never know for sure.

Steve now felt that if such a tragedy struck him and he knew his life was ending, he could handle it well. This was a much different feeling than he had ever had before about life and death. Steve had come to discover the meaning of life. It was not to handle death well; it was not to live life to the fullest each day in case he dies young or because life is short; it was not even being a good person. He would try to do those things, but the meaning of life was in fact to give his life to Christ so that he would know he was going to heaven. This knowledge would prove invaluable for Steve down the strange road he would travel ahead.

September 11, 2001

Anne continually succeeded in her goal of fighting tooth and nail for everything, and employing an army of counselors and social workers to help get her way. The counselors were evaluating the status of Jeff and Eric to help make recommendations about custody. With enough court motions, the divorce case had dragged on in court with several mini-hearings to determine temporary custody and what step would come next.

Steve had been flying to Boston every few months to visit his sons. To his chagrin, these visits were actually evaluated by counselors and reported on to the court. Despite the stupidity of it all, Steve accepted this process, having no other good choice, and he tried to just enjoy his rare moments with his sons. The time had come for his next visit.

Steve woke up early that morning to catch his flight. He looked out his bedroom window and saw that it was snowing. Snowing already, on September 7, at least a month earlier than expected. It wasn't a blizzard, but not just a dusting either. The snow was hard enough to slow down cars on the road, but not hard enough to ground the flights.

Six hours later, Steve's flight landed in Boston. In contrast to Colorado, Boston had temperatures in the high 80's, not just an Indian summer but a heat wave. He couldn't wait to see the boys. It would be the first time in months. Steve wondered to himself if they would look different, and how they would react to seeing him. Several months was a long time for Eric especially, who was still just five years old. The boys were waiting for their dad at Anne's parents' house, where she had dropped them off. Steve pulled into their driveway with great anticipation. He knocked on the door, and heard squeals and running inside. Then the door opened and both boys were there with big smiles on their faces. Steve bent over to hug them, and couldn't even remember exactly what the first thing was that he said. When Eric finally calmed down, he looked outside to the driveway and said, "Where's your car?"

Steve replied, "I flew here in a plane. That's my rental car over there," as he pointed. "Do you like it?"

Eric said, "Yeah, can we go for a ride in it?"

"Sure, a little bit later," Steve said. "Let's do something here first. What would you like to do?" Three minutes later, Steve was sitting on the floor with Eric on his lap reading a story to both boys. It was like they had never been apart, although both boys did look bigger. Steve studied their faces as he read, and he thought about all that had happened since he last saw them.

The visit went well, except for Anne refusing to see Steve. The trip was about seeing Jeff and Eric though, and that was going even better than hoped for. Steve took them to the Children's Museum, on a bike ride, and the like. Steve also enjoyed seeing the sites of Boston again.

On the final scheduled day of the visit, Steve walked into Eric's daycare building to pick him up. All the other boys looked at Steve as he walked in like they had never seen a man before. They asked Eric if that was his dad. He proudly said, "Yes."

The boys had been playing, and it was time to show Steve what they had been doing. One little leader said, "Eric's dad, look at me." He pretended he was a body builder and flexed his muscles. Of course he had very few muscles, so that meant tensing up his arms and shaking them on purpose, their best Arnold Schwarzenegger imitation. Along with the arms was a tense face, and the redder, the better. Soon all the boys copied this as they all repeated, "Eric's dad, look at me." Apparently whoever shook the most won. Yes, Steve's son was growing up. It was funny to see, the type of thing Steve had missed for the last two years.

This was Steve's last day with the boys. It was a fairly short visit since he was scheduled to leave the next day, Tuesday, September 11, 2001. At dinner that night, Steve told them again what they already knew, "I have to leave tomorrow and fly back to Colorado. I'll come back soon to see you again."

"When?" they asked.

Steve told them, "In a few months." Even Eric was now old enough to know that Colorado was a long way away, and that a few months meant a lot more than a few days. He cried as Steve hugged them and said good-bye. The whole trip had gone quite well, but there was still the matter of getting home.

The next morning, Steve woke up to the sound of music on the clock radio. As he was packing up and preparing to leave, a news report came on the TV which he had turned on. He saw video of smoke coming out a tower of the World Trade Center. Steve had been to the top of the World Trade Center years before and always admired the beauty and size of big skyscrapers. He figured this was a minor fire that would be put out quickly so he went about his business. After a shower, Steve walked back in and saw the story on TV continue to unfold. The smoke had not decreased; it had increased significantly. Now there was talk of the possibility that a plane had crashed into the building. It's not far from three airports, but the weather was clear and perfect. How could such a crash have happened under those conditions? Some answers started coming in short order—but they only led to many other questions.

With half the TV cameras in New York now fixed upon the WTC, Steve watched another plane appear from nowhere and slam into the other tower. A fireball engulfed that part of the building for a few seconds. The reporters were largely speechless. The United States was under attack.

Steve's flight wasn't until later that day so he was able to sit uninterrupted and take in the enormity of what was unfolding before the eyes of America. Everybody had seen movies with great special effects of events similar to this, but when it was happening for real, the feeling was quite different. Next came the news of a plane that had crashed into the Pentagon, another building that Steve had been in before.

Then it was back to New York, where things seemed even more critical. Speculation was heard about what else was about to happen. Replays were shown of the second crash. Then came the next big disaster: one tower fell to the ground. Steve watched, unable to fully believe that it was actually happening. This was a huge building. Each tower was bigger than the Empire State Building. Sure, a plane could crash into it and do some damage. It could even start a fire and do more damage. The sprinkler system might even have failed and the fire might have burned for hours, reaching many floors and causing extensive damage, but how could the building possibly collapse? Not the building's engineers and designers, or the fighter pilots that were now in the area, or the president himself could do anything more than watch and hope.

The second tower came down a short while later. As though that wasn't enough, there was also the report of another plane that had crashed in Pennsylvania. Americans had a lot to take in that morning. Steve, like most of the nation, sat mesmerized by the news coverage of events. He heard that all the nation's flights had been grounded. So much for getting home that day. He'd be late returning to work, but who would want to fly that day not knowing what plane was next on the terrorists' hit list?

The afternoon wore on and Steve stayed glued to his TV. He began to hear details about the flights, like what cities they had taken off from and how they were all headed to California. Suddenly it hit Steve that two of the four terrorist teams had taken off from Boston's Logan Airport, where he had landed just days ago. The terrorists had been walking the streets of Boston, New York and Washington for who knows how long, having meetings, getting funding lined up, picking out targets, attending flight training…

Steve's phone rang. It was Jeff. "Hey, Dad, are you okay?"

Suddenly it dawned on Steve that he should have called them earlier. "Yes, I'm still here in Boston," he answered. "Are you watching TV?"

"Yeah," Jeff replied. "Those were big buildings. I feel sorry for those people…You're flying back to Denver when you leave and not going to California, right?"

"Right," he assured him. "I wasn't headed for California today. I used to live there, but I haven't been back since that trip we took to Disneyland."

"I remember that," Jeff said, now sounding greatly relieved. They chatted for a while. Then Jeff got Eric on the phone to talk to Steve. Steve told both of his sons that he loved them. He had always said this fairly often, but today it had more meaning than normal. Finally, Steve asked Eric if he could get Mom and put her on the phone.

Eric said, "Okay," and he put the phone down to go get her. A minute later he returned and said, "She said she doesn't want to talk to you right now."

Steve went to bed that night around midnight. The next day, he turned the TV on when he awoke to see what was new since last night. At noon, it was time to get out of the hotel room where he was staying at Hanscom Air Force Base. Base operations that day were shut down, as were the base's schools. He went for a jog around base housing. Despite being a beautiful September day, and every kid being home from school, base housing was deserted. There was not a kid playing anywhere. Not a moving car anywhere. Even the dogs that were normally out barking at joggers were nowhere to be seen or heard. Were even the kids inside watching the news?

Later that afternoon, Steve went to the nearby mall. On the way, he turned on the radio and found a talk radio station. A caller asked the host, "What is it about us that makes them hate us?" referring to the reason for the attack.

The show's host, normally a cool professional, demonstrated how on edge everybody's nerves still were when he practically shouted, "How can you ask such a thing!" He proceeded to chew out his caller, despite the fact that it was a very reasonable question that was on the minds of many people. In the host's mind, any other answer would have acknowledged that we deserved to be attacked. Chastising the caller somehow seemed like the best reply.

Steve pulled into the mall's parking lot. It was open, but you'd never know it because the place was nearly deserted.

Steve saw a rack of newspaper stands. What the headlines screamed was obvious on this day, but seeing the pictures on the front pages was still astonishing.

The nation's aviation system was still grounded so Steve wasn't leaving town anytime soon. The next day he went to the gym. TV news coverage of the attack was still 24/7, but life was starting to get back to normal and the gym was crowded. As he rode a stationary bike, Steve watched a wall of TVs, every one on a different channel, but all covering the aftermath of the attack. He saw the second plane hit the tower and the towers come down a hundred times. He was also now seeing reports from the Middle East of people dancing and celebrating what had happened here.

Then Steve spotted someone he recognized. It was Phil Roberts, an old friend from Steve's military days. He walked over to Phil, who recognized Steve immediately. They shook hands and talked about the topic of the day.

"Can you believe what they did to us?" asked Phil.

Steve responded, "No, it's still pretty hard to believe. They don't know what they're doing."

"What do you mean?" Phil asked.

Steve explained, "They say that foreigners like our culture but hate our government. They like our jeans, music, movies and food, but they attacked us because they hate our government's policies. Now it's true that our government has turned into a bunch of incompetent liars who can't balance their own checkbook, let alone the national budget—but foreigners don't care about that. The big picture is that they won't accept how our governmental system enables democracy, technology and capitalism. That's how we left them in the dust economically, socially and militarily. That's what they should be fighting for in their own country. They're not going to fix their problems by attacking us."

Steve hadn't realized how much the attack had affected him until this moment. "Here's the key—their governments and citizens are badly disconnected. Their governments are dictatorships. Most of their citizens know of our freedom and democracy and want it for themselves, but those few elite dictators in control sacrifice progress to keep themselves in power and keep their own people afraid of doing anything to enable change that might drag them out of the 7th century. They do all they can to keep democracy away. All attempts at starting competing political parties are crushed. They brainwash their children to hate us, and it works. That's why they're willing to fight us."

Steve continued, his opinions seeming to solidify as he spoke. "Then there's our culture. Our freedom and prosperity don't necessarily lead to virtue or morals. It used to, but look at the choices we make these days. We're materialistic. Divorce is destroying the family. Gays are now accepted and encouraged, especially in this state. They even make TV shows for them and elect them to office. Next thing you know, they'll be legalizing gay marriage. Sodom and Gomorrah got destroyed for less than that. Prisons are jam packed. Have you heard any rap lyrics lately? Then there's pornography. It's exploding thanks to the internet, same with gambling. People's biggest concern is if they have enough beer for the game each weekend."

Phil walked over to a nearby bike, and then finally responded, "That doesn't mean we should be getting attacked."

"I agree," Steve responded. "I just hope we use this as a wake up call, not to roll over or give in, but to get our nation back on track. We can start by being grateful that things weren't even worse two days ago."

"How could things have been worse?" Phil asked.

"Easy," Steve replied. "It could have been 11 planes like

they planned to blow up over the Pacific a few years ago. Or those four planes could have had five times as many passengers on them. Back in '93 when they bombed the World Trade Center, their plan was to topple over one tower in the direction of the other and get them both to fall. It almost worked. They say it could have killed 250,000."

Then Phil yelled out one of his favorite words with a big grin and laugh, not caring who else was around to hear it.

Steve wondered if he should say it, and then he did, not sure what tone to say it with. "In case you never knew, that's why we called you 'Filthy Phil.' I mean, do you say that around your kids? That's another thing—we have a culture that we should shelter our kids from, but we don't even have enough sense to do that."

Steve hated to press an issue like this, but the events of two days ago made it seem like the time had come to do so. He felt good that he had made the point he wanted and didn't even remember what Phil said in response.

The next day was Friday, September 14, and the FAA finally announced that the airports would reopen the next morning. By then, many people had changed their travel plans. Many trips, both business and pleasure, now seemed unneeded and had been cancelled. Many other people had decided to drive instead of fly. Steve was one of a handful of people who had to get home but was too far away to justify driving. He called the airline and got on a flight scheduled to leave at 9:00 AM the next morning.

Steve wasn't quite sure what to expect, but he knew it wouldn't be a normal day or a normal flight. He got to the airport around 7:30. Security was tighter than normal, but there were also fewer passengers than normal, so checking in didn't take too long. That was the good news; then came the bad news: his flight would be at least two hours late. Steve asked if there was a mechanical problem. He was told no, but the agent did not know the reason—not that he was saying at least.

Steve headed for the gate. All the things he took for granted at an airport were suddenly more noticeable. There certainly were more guards than normal. It seemed everybody was looking at everybody else to give them the once over. Steve got to the gate to wait and pulled out a book to read.

Half an hour later things started buzzing. There were people milling about everywhere—not fellow travelers, but airport employees. Suddenly news crews began appearing with lights and TV cameras. Steve looked out the window and saw a plane taxiing toward him. Come to think of it, it was the first plane he had seen or heard moving all day. Steve observed out the window that the aircraft's path was literally lined by workers on the ramp in their many baggage vehicles and food trucks who had ceremoniously lined up to usher in the airport's first arrival. The plane pulled up to the gate where Steve was.

Inside the terminal, applause broke out with the appearance of the first passenger. It kept up for everyone as they deplaned. Steve watched each person as they walked into the terminal. First were the passengers, just a dozen or so. Then came several airline employees. Apparently this flight was mostly a repositioning of a plane and flight crews. Some of the last stewardesses that came off were in tears. Here were people who flew daily for a living, and even they had a reaction like this!

Two hours later, Steve's flight was finally ready to go. He wondered what had he gotten into as he got ready to get on the plane. Should he have taken the train as someone suggested? It was now obvious that the airline operations would take hours if not days to get back to normal. After an airport gets snowed in and shuts down for a day, there are huge crowds the next morning jamming every plane. That was not the case here though. For now, there were fewer planes than normal in the skies to accidentally crash into. There was a higher level of security inspections than ever. There were nineteen fewer terrorists alive than a few days ago to try to hijack another plane. Steve's flight had only a handful of people on it and was probably the safest flight in the history of aviation, yet you couldn't convince Steve or his fellow passengers of that.

After taking off and getting up to altitude, everyone finally relaxed. Three hours later at the airport in Denver, a major hub, Steve noticed again that this large airport had very few people in it even though it was rush hour. Only on Christmas Day had Steve ever seen it so empty.

Steve had been on better trips and worse trips than the one he just completed, but he had never been on a trip as strange as this one. The world had changed in the past week; things were not the same anymore. What would happen in the days and weeks ahead? For one thing, Steve would come much closer to terrorism than he had that week in Boston.

STARTING OVER;
BIN LADEN PREPARES

Back home, Steve quickly returned to his daily routine, but it didn't last long. The day soon came for Steve's long-awaited last trip to court to finalize the divorce and custody arrangement. Anne had to fly back to Colorado for this court appearance as she had done for each of the several previous mini-hearings that led up to this one. After an all–day affair in front of a judge, the divorce mess was finally over and done with, but things didn't go well for Steve, and he was quite depressed.

A couple days later, Steve was feeling better. He was better able to talk about the court results when he ran into Mary at work. They had lunch together. "How did it go?" Mary asked.

"Well, I got about nothing I asked for. She unilaterally broke a legally binding marriage contract, yet everybody bends over backwards to help her and give her what she wants. If I move to Boston, then I'll still only get the boys every other weekend."

"That's too bad," Mary replied. "Are you going to move there?"

"Probably. Everything is pushing me that way. I have to sell the house to give her half the proceeds."

"That's the right thing to do," Mary said. "You should have moved there long ago."

"It will be weird for Jeff and Eric to spend time with me if I move there. Anne and I have very different parenting styles. She was raised by very rigid, structured parents; mine were the opposite. We each turned out to be just like our parents. She'd be a good military drill sergeant because she's very rules-oriented, very by-the-book, and she has a very thick book."

Mary laughed, and then added, "By the way, parenting every other weekend is what dad's often get, so there's nothing to feel bad about."

They talked a while longer. Steve eventually said, "I haven't seen you in a couple of weeks. What's new with you?"

There was news, and he would be sorry he asked. "I got orders," Mary replied. "I'm getting reassigned to a base in Virginia."

Steve knew this day was coming. Mary had been due for reassignment for awhile. Steve had already told her previously that he would miss her when that day came and she left town. He had thought about how sad and strange it would be to not see her anymore. "How soon do you leave?" he asked.

"In about three weeks."

Steve knew this was good news for Mary. She had been ready to leave and end this chapter of her life, quite similar to Steve's situation.

During the next week, Steve decided he needed the same thing; it was time for him to move. He didn't really need that last nudge he had gotten from Mary. He hadn't enjoyed his job much at the Academy. He thought he could get a job at least that good in the Boston area. He had to sell the house anyway. Terry was no longer around. Mary would be gone soon. He had bad memories of Colorado Springs. His kids were in Boston, and that was where he belonged. Eric had cried each time Steve visited when he left on the final day and said good-bye. Steve had wondered every time why he wasn't already moving there.

Mary stopped by to say good-bye the day before she left town. This was the first time Steve could recall that he didn't enjoy seeing her. She was not as emotional in her good-bye as Steve was, but that's because Steve had more emotions wrapped up in her than she did in him. They each said they intended to stay in touch. Steve knew he would try to do so, but he was not as sure about her. He sadly watched her drive off.

After finishing his own moving preparations a month later, Steve left town himself. At this point he was ready to put Colorado in his rear view mirror. He had a long drive ahead of him with lots of time to think. He couldn't help but think often about how he had arrived in Colorado several years ago with a wife and kids, but he was now leaving all by himself. He now had no marriage, no wife, no house, no job, and only barely felt like he had any kids. To top it off, things hadn't really worked out with Mary as he had hoped either.

During his long drive, Steve had a chance to put things into perspective. 9–11 had a way of doing that for everyone. Steve listened to many radio news reports and talk shows as he drove. The topic was usually 9–11 and what might happen next. He heard stories about al-Qaeda possibly having obtained as many as forty nuclear weapons from the former Soviet Union nations and on the black market. Bin Laden may have been paying nuclear scientists from Russia and Pakistan to maintain this arsenal, and to assemble additional weapons he procured. There was speculation that some nukes had already been planted in the U.S. some years ago by the Soviet Union during the Cold War. Al-Qaeda may have been paying former Russian experts to assist them in locating these nuclear weapons.

Were plans underway for an attack that would make 9–11 pale in comparison; an enormous blow against the U.S. which is seen by al-Qaeda as the Great Satan?

All this seemed possible. Bin Laden could afford this since he had nearly unlimited funds to spend on a nuclear terrorism plan because he was in control of the Afghanistan heroin industry. Production was increasing greatly. Al-Qaeda had developed close relations with those who smuggle and sell the heroin throughout Europe and the U.S. Bin Laden's personal wealth was said to be at least $300 million.

Some high level U.S. officials believed some nuclear weapons had been smuggled into the U.S. for use in up to seven major cities as part of a plan dubbed "American Hiroshima." CIA Director George Tenet informed President Bush one month after Sept. 11, 2001, that at least two suitcase nukes had reached al-Qaeda operatives in the U.S., each capable of producing a blast of between two and ten kilotons. This prompted President Bush to order his national security team to give nuclear terrorism top priority over every other threat. Bush also ordered the building of underground bunkers for use by federal government managers following such an attack. Inexplicably though, Bush and his team failed to secure the U.S. - Mexico border through which weapons and al-Qaeda operatives were believed to be passing.

As he drove across the country, Steve contemplated all this. Maybe it wasn't meant to work with Anne, plus he didn't have the doubts of being the one who filed for divorce. In fact, maybe she had done him a favor—the arguing and stress had started to hurt Steve's health. Then right when he really needed a friend, he met Mary. She was able to help him like no male friend could have. She got his mind off Anne often. This also taught Steve that he could fall in love again. Additionally, what if he and Mary had hooked up romantically? They were both destined to leave for different places so it may have ultimately been even sadder if they had developed a relationship.

Maybe things had worked out perfectly for Steve, as though someone was watching out for him. After all, through all of the pain and turmoil he had come to know God, and made a good friend in Mary.

The more hours and days Steve drove, the more excited he got about what lay ahead for him. It would be good to get to Boston, to be a father again and see much more of Jeff and Eric, and to start over with a new job. He was still a young man who had a lot going for him, and a lot did lie ahead for him. In fact, 9–11 had started a chain of events that would lead to much more in the years ahead.

THE SECOND BIGGEST PRIZE

Steve was confident he was doing the right thing during his cross-country drive. He pulled into Boston with great anticipation and a quiet confidence that he was doing the right things to improve his life.

He got an apartment on the outskirts of Boston near Hanscom Air Force Base. He knew this part of town quite well since had been had been stationed at Hanscom years ago. He also figured he was as likely to get a job there as anywhere. Hanscom was just west of Boston, in the suburb of Lexington. Lexington's history as the sight of the famous "shot heard round the world" was well-known and led to a Revolutionary War battle. Boston itself had many major attractions like the Freedom Trail, Bunker Hill, the USS Constitution, and Steve's favorite baseball team, the Red Sox. He was excited to be back.

Steve's plan was to spend a week unpacking and then start looking for a job. Jeff and Eric came for the weekend during that first week. They helped with the unpacking. At one point, Eric sat on a box to rest. The box instantly started to make a loud noise that startled him so he jumped off.

"What's that, Dad?!"

"Let's check it out!"

The noise ended quickly, and a little investigation showed that he had accidentally caused a fire extinguisher to discharge—maybe "explode" would be a better description. Everything in the box was ruined and thrown out.

"Sorry, Dad."

"No big deal," Steve said. "Could have been worse."

The boys took notice of this, since they had been ready for a worse reaction from their father than that. Steve had mellowed, and didn't let the small stuff bother him anymore.

Steve dropped off the boys at their schools on Monday morning. He enjoyed this chance to become much more a part of their lives, to see their schools and wish them well at school that day, and best of all, Eric wasn't sad when he said good-bye that morning. He knew his dad was going to be nearby for now on.

Steve started looking for a job later that week. It took a month, but he found a job that seemed tailor made for him—he would be an engineer on the Missile Defense System at Hanscom AFB. This was the new name of the program that had started in 1983 under President Ronald Reagan. Back then it was called the Strategic Defense Initiative, and nicknamed Star Wars. The original plan back then was to build a huge network of satellites, sensors and even space-based weapons capable of thwarting a massive missile strike launched by the Soviet Union or China.

The network had never really panned out in those early years due to its technical complexity. Then the Cold War ended, Reagan left office, and the program floundered under the next two presidents as its uncertain future was re-examined. More recently, President Bush resurrected the program with this new name and a more limited role. The new, scaled-down mission was to build a system that could shoot down a single missile or small number of missiles launched by rogue nations like Iran or North Korea who might develop or buy such weapons.

With his engineering background and experience on similar programs while on active duty, Steve was placed on the engineering design team. He was a civil servant again, like he had been at the Air Force Academy, but now he was much more in his element. This was what he knew how to do and enjoyed.

Steve became good friends with one of his co-workers named Howard. They got along well at work and got together sometimes away from work. They talked about many things, such as the war.

It was now 2003, and the U.S. had been at war in Afghanistan for a year and a half and had recently elevated things by going into Iraq as well. One day at lunch Steve asked Howard, "Why do you think we went into Iraq?"

Howard thought and then responded, "I think it was a number of reasons. First there are the weapons of mass destruction, the advertised reason. We haven't found them yet, but it certainly seems they existed. We know Hussein used them consistently in the 80's against Iran and even used them on his own people. He didn't suddenly lose them, did he?"

Steve smiled and said, "Well, if he did, it's because he buried them or sent them to someplace like Syria to hide them."

Then Howard continued. "Then comes the possibly bigger and unadvertised reason."

"Oil?" asked Steve.

"Indirectly," Howard responded. "Bush is not there to take over the oilfields or oil supply. However, Saddam Hussein had snubbed the U.S. by no longer accepting U.S. dollars as payment for oil shipments. Too much of that and the world might not accept the U.S. dollar as the world currency anymore. That may have been the straw that broke the camel's back."

"I've read about that," Steve said as he thought about it. "If that's part of the equation, I could see that they would have to keep quiet about it. Any reason other than self defense would not be acceptable, so they gambled that WMDs would be adequate justification."

"On top of that," Howard added, "Hussein had called on all Arab countries to impose an oil embargo on the U.S. in retaliation for the UN sanctions."

Then Steve changed the topic, "Do you think we're at war with terrorists or Muslims?"

"Good question," Howard replied. "My take on it is that we're at war with Islam. It's a religion that teaches followers to convert people and kill those that won't submit. Fortunately, most of them ignore that part of Islam even if they believe it. I guess the ones we're at war with are the relatively few who completely follow their religion."

Steve added, "Relatively few of a billion people is still a lot of people."

Everybody had heard much about Islam since 9–11. Howard had done extensive reading on the subject, and he continued. "I've read that Muslim men are allowed to marry up to four wives, have unlimited sex slaves, and beat and kill an unruly wife. They made up some god named Allah. Then there's Allah's prophet, Mohammed, who broke his own man-made law and had fifteen wives, including one he married at age sixty when she was ten. One of their five pillars is that there is no god but Allah. They say the Trinity—God as Father, Son and Holy Ghost—is blasphemous and its believers go to hell. They say Jesus was nothing but a human teacher and prophet. They deny his death and resurrection for our sins. It's the most anti-Christian religion on earth, and the most violent, too. It started out based upon intimidation, violence and murder, and it's still that way today. Most Muslims seem unaware that their ancestors were forced into Islam under threat of death. Those that know their history seem proud of it…That's what we're up against."

Steve had been waiting to ask a question. "Did you see the piece they did on 60 *Minutes* last night?"

"Yes," Howard said. "It was striking. They confirmed most of what I have read but at first found hard to believe. Muslims base their lives and their future on the Quran, which is nothing but man-made propaganda. Conversely, the Bible states that it's the inspired word of God, and then proved it with hundreds of prophecies that came true. Islam doesn't have a book with that track record. Early parts of the Quran even state that the God of the Jews is the true God, says the Jews are God's chosen people, and says God gave them the Promised Land. Elsewhere it says the opposite, so it's very inconsistent. It goes on to command every Muslim to participate in jihad of an offensive and unlimited nature."

The year 2004 was a very good and eventful year for Steve. Things were going well in Boston with his job and children. At work, the program was continuing development of the Missile Defense System. It was a very complicated piece of technology that was being developed. Progress came slowly; slowly enough that successful milestones seemed to be few and far between. Part of the problem was that the team could only estimate if they were close to success. Tests were infrequent due to the cost and risk of what they were doing, and they could only partially test capabilities in a non-real world test environment. Another problem was all the man-hours that had to go into convincing headquarters in Washington that the system would work and was worth the cost. This included endless briefings to the Washington brass with cost and schedule updates.

One day that fall Steve was at work when a co-worker, Liz, invited him to go to a club after work and he accepted. Once there, they looked around the room for anybody else they knew. Liz said she saw somebody and pointed. Steve looked and could not believe his eyes. It was Mary.

Steve had run into some people still in the Hanscom area from when he lived here previously, but hadn't dreamed of seeing Mary. He hadn't seen her in three years, but suddenly that changed in a big way. Mary then noticed Steve and got a smile on her face, just like he had on his. She walked over and they embraced. Mary had spent three years in Virginia and was then reassigned to Hanscom. Just by coincidence, Mary had met Liz since her recent arrival.

Steve barely knew where to start as the three of them talked. He found out that Mary had arrived just a couple of weeks ago. Mary said she hoped Steve was still in the Boston area and she was going to try to look him up soon, but they had lost track of each other. The three sat and talked and laughed for an hour before they had to leave to get home.

There was a lot to say and ask that Steve didn't have a chance to get to, but he did find out that Mary worked on base nearby. She had also not remarried. This surprised Steve, not that he minded.

Steve and Mary started getting together again, some-times with friends like Liz, and sometimes just the two of them. They did some dating-like activities like they had in Colorado. They still had a lot in common and now even had a history together from Colorado. While having dinner one night together at her house, Mary asked Steve, "Have you dated much since you moved here?"

Steve was surprised to hear that question, but responded, "Some, but nothing that's worked out or lasted too long."

Mary sighed. "I've met some losers. I could write a book on that topic."

"Sometimes I wonder how I ever got married once," said Steve. It takes so much for two people to be compatible enough to last a lifetime, and even if one thinks it could work, the other might not."

I've had that same thought," Mary said. "I didn't think I'd get divorced, and I thought I'd get remarried by now, but I don't want to rush into a panic marriage."

Steve's feelings for Mary had been rekindled since meeting her again a couple of weeks ago. He daydreamed about her a lot, and now wondered if he should say something, or just kiss her. He leaned over. She seemed to see it coming and seemed all right with that, so he kissed her and made it more than a quick peck. It could be said that the kiss was four years in the making, and it felt worth the wait to Steve. Mary felt good also. Three years was enough time to change lives and perspectives, and apparently it had done so for her.

They talked a while longer that evening. When saying good night at the door, Steve said with a bit of a chuckle, "I guess tonight turned into a date at some point."

Mary smiled and said, "Seems that way…Let's do more of this."

Steve was crazy about Mary again.

They continued to date and the relationship blossomed. After several months, Steve felt like it was the right moment to propose. One night after dinner, Steve held Mary's hand and said, "Mary, I never really forgot about you those three years we were apart. I missed you. I love being with you. I love talking to you. I love doing things with you. I love thinking about you, which I do all the time. I love you. Will you marry me?"

He knew Mary was ready to get married to the right man. He knew she was the one for him, but wasn't totally sure what she thought. Had he rushed things? He had a habit of being too optimistic.

Mary smiled and said, "Yes."

They planned the marriage for that summer. Mary and her mother planned most of the wedding. Steve's only request was that his favorite song be sung during the ceremony.

Summer came and so did the wedding day, a beautiful day. As Steve stood in the church watching Mary walk down the aisle, he recalled a story from his divorce recovery class. Someone in his group of ten people had asked if anyone had any doubts on their wedding day. Of that group of ten, eight said they had. Steve was one of only two that didn't, but he still wound up divorced. He had been optimistic that day, as he usually was. He was optimistic again on this day. This time he had even more reason to be so. He and Mary were best friends. They were great for each other. They complimented each other well. They were equally yoked. They had not rushed into a second marriage. They were both ready for this. Mary had tears in her eyes when she heard the singing of what was also one of her favorite songs:

> Let there be peace on earth,
> and let it begin with me.
> Let there be peace on Earth,
> the peace that was meant to be.

With God as our Father,
brothers all are we,
Let me walk with my brother,
in perfect harmony.

Let peace begin with me,
let this be the moment now.
With every step I take,
let this be my solemn vow,

To take each moment and live each moment
in peace, eternally.
Let there be Peace on Earth,
and let it begin with me.

———————————————

Osama bin Laden had now been a much-sought after fugitive for many years as he lived in the caves of Pakistan and Afghanistan. He lived a simple life, sleeping on cots and eating plain foods. However, this did not mean that he was unable to function. He continued to effectively meet with his network and plan further terrorist actions. When he moved from place to place, it was in a convoy of 10–20 trucks filled with bodyguards pledged to die for him.

The day after Steve and Mary's marriage came another terrorist attack. A series of coordinated terrorist bomb blasts hit London's public transport system during the morning rush hour of July 7, 2005. Three bombs exploded within one minute of each other on three London subway trains. A fourth bomb exploded on a bus an hour later. The bombings killed fifty-two commuters and the four suicide bombers, injured another seven hundred, and caused a severe day-long disruption of the city's transport and communications infrastructure nationwide. This very success-ful attack reminded the world that Osama bin Laden and al-Qaeda were not helplessly hiding in a cave somewhere, and that America was not their only target. The world was becoming a more dangerous place, and peace was getting harder and harder to come by.

THE HOLY LAND CALLS

The wars in Iraq and Afghanistan were still going on and were already longer than planned. There were thirty-eight countries that supplied troops to the war efforts. Only three European countries voted against the Iraq war, and all three of them were involved in the well-known United Nations Oil for Food scandal. The war was getting bad publicity and the U.S. public was getting impatient, but the war was going on over there, not on U.S. soil, and there was no draft. For most American citizens the war was nothing more than something to talk about. The war was not thought of as World War III, but the label rung true—the scope and impact of the war were huge and still growing.

Steve and Mary were not average citizens, though, relegated to war updates on the nightly news. Mary was an active duty military officer, and Steve was still working on a major new defense system. They both understood the place this war was having in world history as it raged on. It had done so now for six years in Afghanistan and four years in Iraq.

The year 2007 was important for Steve and the Missile Defense System since they had a major test scheduled. Since President Reagan launched the U.S. missile defense program in 1983, which envisioned an impregnable missile shield over the U.S. to protect the country from missile attack, $91 billion had been spent, with $58 billion more slated to be spent over the next six years. As the technology challenge of building a missile shield turned out to be far more daunting than originally thought, the cost climbed. In a series of scripted tests from 1999 to 2005 costing $100 million each, interceptor missiles had destroyed dummy warheads in just five out of ten tries.

Shooting down a missile is no walk in the park. As the interceptor and target missiles approach each other at six miles a second, the smallest problem meant failure. A 2002 test failed after the interceptor didn't separate from its booster. The reason: A single pin on a tiny integrated circuit broke after being violently shaken during the flight. Foam that had been there to protect the pin on prior flights had been removed, supposedly to improve the system's reliability. A 2004 test failed because an error in one line of computer code kept the interceptor grounded. The most recent failure, in February 2005, happened after two of the three arms that held the interceptor in place in its silo didn't fully retract during launch because a part had corroded.

It was now time for the latest test, and everybody was watching. Steve traveled out to Vandenberg AFB, California, to monitor the test. The plan was for an interceptor missile to be launched from Vandenberg and shoot down a target missile fired from Alaska that resembled a North Korean missile.

The crucial test was successful, as the interceptor hit and destroyed the target missile in space over the Pacific Ocean. This was a step in the right direction; however, the test lacked realism in two significant ways. First, it was scripted. In a real-life attack, the timing, trajectory and characteristics of an incoming missile would not be known ahead of time like they had been in this test. Second, the target missile did not deploy decoys or other countermeasures meant to confuse the interceptor missile from striking the actual warhead. Deploying decoys was simple technically and would probably be done in real life.

The main objective had been to allow the Missile Defense Agency to claim the program was back on track after the interceptors in the last two flight tests in 2004 and 2005 failed to even leave their silos and get airborne. The program needed success in this test to proceed and seek further funding. This successful test would probably enable that.

It had been a quick test of only about twelve minutes from launch to impact. The time-consuming part came before the launch with all the preparation, and afterwards with mountains of telemetry and other data to review and analyze.

Steve felt good when he left the test monitor facility later that day to head for the hotel, but not as good as the others felt. As he walked to his car, he saw a TV camera crew approaching him. He had seen them over the years, and knew that they often appeared after a launch since the whole nearby town heard, saw and even felt most missile launches. Steve had never been interviewed himself, but had been briefed on how to handle himself if it should happen. He also knew the program well, both its history as well as what had happened today. He felt he could be a good spokesman, should they want to talk to him.

They did. Newswoman Cindy Newman introduced herself to Steve and asked if she could interview him about the launch. Steve agreed. The cameraman, Randy Bomar, introduced himself to Steve. The three chatted in preparation for the interview. Five minutes later, the camera was rolling. Cindy recapped the day's events, then turned to Steve and asked him for his reaction.

Steve said, "Well, we passed the test today, but the result is only so-so. We passed because the test was not that rigorous, not very realistic in the real world. We have a long way to go. We're at war and at a point in history when the country needs this system working to counter the threat. We need to get the necessary funding to speed up progress."

Steve flew home later that week. He had missed Mary and was glad to get back home to see her. They had an enjoyable, if uneventful, weekend together.

Steve was back at the office at Hanscom on Monday when he got called into the office of his boss, Colonel Forbrick. The colonel seemed serious as he said, "Steve, there was a problem at the test site last week."

Steve replied, "Yeah, a few technical hiccups, but we found the problem in the telemetry and have it fixed already."

"No, I don't mean that," he continued. "There was a major problem with the interview you did with KTLA-TV."

"I was cleared by Public Affairs to do that," Steve said in his defense.

"Right," the colonel said. "But that doesn't mean you can say anything you want. You said the wrong thing, and you said it to the wrong station."

"What do you mean by the wrong station?"

"KTLA is not from the little beach town down the road that nobody would have seen. KTLA is the largest station in Los Angeles. You were seen by many, and seen by someone who complained."

Steve said, "I'm sorry, but I'm not sure what to be sorry for. Every word I said was accurate."

"I've seen the tape," Colonel Forbrick said, "and you're right about that, but this is a big bucks program—and that makes it a political program. Steve, the wrong person saw the interview, and he wants a head to roll. I'm sorry, and you don't deserve this because you're a valuable asset to the program, but we have to let you go."

There was silence for a moment, and then Steve asked, "Who did that directive come from? Was it the Pentagon?"

"No. I assume the Pentagon has seen the interview, but they didn't complain. It came from higher than that—a senator on the Armed Forces Budget Committee. He just happened to see the interview and was put off."

Steve jumped in, "I don't even know what I said wrong. What didn't he like?"

"Your budget comment. There are channels for appropriations requests. He doesn't want pressure from the media. And that was preceded by your remark about results not being more positive. I think that got him going. Anyway, there is some good news in this." Steve perked up. "With your background, there are opportunities out there for you. I'm sure you can get a job with a contractor."

Steve thanked the colonel and left in short order.

Steve had been given a transcript of the interview and read it several times. They were right—he could have chosen his words better and he did come across the wrong way. Steve had never been good at verbal tip-toeing or political games.

Steve felt bad for himself and his family. He knew it had been just one person who caused his dismissal, along with just being in the wrong place at the wrong time. He had done a very good job for the program for almost six years since moving back to Massachusetts. The previous test setbacks had not been his fault. His engineering capabilities were top-notch. Additionally, his budget background from Colorado had enabled him to help the program's budgeting

department with crucial decisions that had improved esti-
mates and saved some embarrassment. It all seemed unfair.

Steve got home early that day. He loved this job and
knew he would miss it, but he now had the tools to deal
with this career setback. He remembered Proverbs 16:3–4:
"Commit to the Lord whatever you do and your plans will
succeed. The Lord works out everything for his own ends."

Steve gave Mary the news that night when she got home.
All the more ironic in this situation was that she worked in
Public Affairs and had experience herself in TV interviews
in which she was quite gifted. They talked at length about
things. Their marriage was strong, and that gave Steve even
more means to help him recover quickly that day.

A few days later, Steve had just begun looking for a new
job when Mary came home with some news of her own.
"Steve, guess what?" she asked. "I'm not sure if it's good or
bad news, but I got reassignment orders."

"Already? It hasn't even been three years yet," Steve said.

"With the war and all that's going on, resources get
stretched thin and things get sped up sometimes."

"So, where to?" Steve inquired.

"It's a big one. An overseas assignment to Israel," she said.

"Israel?" Steve said. "We don't even have a military
base there."

"It's an assignment to the U.S. Embassy in Tel Aviv,
Israel. They need a Communications and Public Affairs
Officer and my name came up. Personnel told me I couldn't
talk my way out of this assignment if I tried, and I don't
think I want to try. It sounds exciting to me. We've talked
about something like this, Steve, and we knew it might be

coming. It's different. It's exciting. Plus it's safer than Iraq right now, which is where they could have sent me."

"Although Israel and Lebanon were at war last year, and Iran's president has publicly threatened many times to blow Israel off the face of the earth," Steve added, reluctant to put his wife in that level of danger.

"But at least it's not a war zone, not right now," Mary replied.

Steve admired her attitude. He recalled the time he told Anne that they might get assigned to a base in Utah and she reacted by saying, "Who wants to be around all those Mormons?"

Conversely, and typical of Mary, here she was all set to go to a vastly different environment with seemingly no reservations.

Steve told her, "Years ago I took a flight from Athens to Bangkok, Thailand. I could not get over that I was flying over these exotic places like the Arabian Sea and India and the Bay of Bengal. I was also over Israel, but that got no attention from me back then. Now the place fascinates me…Let's go. We'll make it work."

Steve and Mary were still practically newlyweds and the thought of her going alone was never really considered by either of them. Moving would have been harder if Steve had to quit the Missile Defense Program, but that was no longer a problem. He just assumed he could get a job there as easily as here.

They had a month to prepare for the move. The only problem seemed to be their children. After much discussion, they decided to leave the younger boys, Mary's son and Steve's younger son Eric, stateside with their other parent. Steve's older son Jeff had just finished high school and was still trying to decide between joining the military or going to college. He was presented the option of going with Steve and Mary for a possibly once-in-a-lifetime opportunity to live overseas. This would also give him a chance to delay his military or college decision a year or two or until he was more sure of his decision. He decided to go.

Just in case, Mary and Steve updated their wills. This pushed Steve into a discussion he had meant to have with Mary. One day he sat down with her and began. "Mary, remember that day back in 2000 when we were talking in the hallway at work and I told you about investing?"

"Vaguely," she recalled.

"Have you followed the markets any since then?"

Mary answered, "Everything's up, right? Stocks, bonds, real estate?"

"Sort of," Steve said, "but investments seem to go in these ten-year cycles. Gold and oil and inflation hedges did great in the 70's. Japan stocks did great in the 80's. U.S. stocks did great in the 90's. When U.S. stocks cratered in 2000–2001, it signaled the next change back to gold." He paused and then asked, "Remember I told you the government was manipulating the price of gold?"

"I remember that. Were they?"

"Yes, there's even proof. Remember Alan Greenspan at the Fed? He actually said in testimony to the U.S. Senate Banking Committee in 1998 that the Central Banks were ready to lease gold should the need arise. Translation—we're taking gold down, and they did, so much so that people no longer invested 5–10% of their savings in it like they used to. They called gold a 'barbarous relic' whose time was over, but they were wrong. Gold has been valuable for 6,000 years because it's rare, unlike paper money. It's not going out of business, and its time had come again. It's been going up ever since."

Mary asked, "Isn't it close to its all-time high?"

"It's close, yet it's getting no attention. That means it's no where near the end of its run yet. All you have to do is see one of these multi-year runs coming once in your life and you can make a fortune. Since the tech stock drop of 2000, stocks are up maybe 70% while gold is up 200% and gold mining company stocks are up about 800%. The blow-off climb that always comes at the end hasn't even happened yet."

"Wow," Mary said. "But why would they manipulate prices? Isn't that illegal?"

"It's illegal if any person or brokerage house does it, but the government and Fed think they're entitled so they don't hesitate. What's worse is that they don't do it for the public's benefit. They do it for themselves. They can control the amount of dollars in circulation and they want the public's wealth held in dollars because that gives them power. Remember what we did in 2003 when Iraq stopped accepting dollars for oil transactions? We attacked! Earlier this year, Iran did the same thing. Now they only accept European Euros, and they're encouraging other nations to do the same thing. It's really an economic war. Terrorist tapes have even included them shouting, 'The dollar is dead.'"

"And since then," Mary injected, "the U.S. saber rattling has increased. It's not about oil; it's about the almighty dollar."

Two weeks after Mary got orders, she and Steve were still preparing for their move when news was all over the airwaves of Iran being bombed. Who had done so? Was this the beginning of a protracted war to include a ground invasion? The news coverage was extensive, and it was quickly reported that the Israeli Air Force had launched a single wave of bombing runs on selected Iranian sites being used for their nuclear development program. Both Israel and the U.S. administrations had felt for months that this was a justified and necessary event for two reasons. First, Iran had ignored United Nations sanctions against their nuclear development. Second, and bigger yet, Iran had repeatedly threatened Israel and the United States with total annihilation.

What wasn't stated publicly was that the U.S. was not in a position to do much about this, due to being preoccupied and bogged down with the war in Iraq, and because there was much opposition at home to any such move of war escalation. Israel, on the other hand, was the nation that was targeted for destruction even more than the U.S. Israel is also much closer geographically to Iran and is a much smaller country which makes it much more vulnerable. The Israeli cabinet felt they could not wait around to be attacked on the enemy's terms, quite possibly with nuclear weapons no less, but must instead take steps to prevent that.

Part of the reason for this action by Israel was that they privately had the support and backing of their ally, the U.S. In fact, the U.S. supplied the 5,000 pound bombs used by Israeli planes to hit the underground sites. It had been many bunker-busting bombs that were used, precision guided by Global Positioning Satellites for pinpoint accuracy. Facilities in six Iranian cities were hit: Tehran, Natanz, Tabriz, Arak, Fasa and Darkhovin. Iran had purposely spread its facilities around its country to make such an attack harder.

Predictably, the world condemned Israel for its action even though any country would have done the same thing to protect itself (except maybe France). The same thing had happened in 1981 when Israel bombed a nuclear reactor in Iraq and successfully destroyed it. Israel had the courage and skill to rid the world of Iraq's threat temporarily, yet the world's media condemned Israel as though it had committed a war crime. Time even went on to prove the hostile intentions of Saddam Hussein and the necessity of what

Israel had done because when the Persian Gulf War commenced a decade later in 1991, the world had Israel to thank for preventing Iraq from being a nuclear power. Israel had made a quick victory possible. Yet even with that lesson in mind, the world was again showing its short-sightedness and expressing anger toward Israel for no valid reason.

At first, many people were afraid the bombing would lead Israel right into war with Iran. After a few days though, neither side had taken any further action. This strengthened the position of Israel's still new Prime Minister, Ehud Olmert. The whole crisis was out of the news in America before too long.

These events made Steve and Mary feel that living in Israel would be even safer since Iran now seemed to be weaker and less likely to follow through on their previous threats, due to Israel's bombing. Part of the reason for Iran's inaction was that the U.S. had three aircraft carriers in the Persian Gulf region to help deter retaliation.

Before they knew it, moving day had arrived for the Van de Kamps. Mary and Steve had each moved many times in their lives, but this one was different. This time they were going overseas. That meant flying there while their goods were shipped by boat, including their car.

When their long flight took off from Boston for Tel Aviv, Jeff wondered if he was doing the right thing. He had a long conversation with his dad and step mom on the flight centering on the state of Israel. He asked them, "It seems like everyone makes fun of Jews, and many people hate them. Why?"

"It sure seems that way," Mary replied. "The country has a strange and long history, very long. It says in Genesis

15:18 that God promised land to Abraham and his descendants from Egypt to the Euphrates River. Today though, Israel has only about 10% of that land; the rest is owned by Lebanon, Syria, Jordan, Iraq and Saudi Arabia. You'd think those neighbors would be happy with that, but instead, Arabs accuse Israel of stealing the remaining 10% from them. Israel settles for the 10% and tries to live in peace but keeps getting attacked. They get blamed for starting wars when they don't. Leaders of neighboring nations keep lying about Israel and feel that if they do it long enough and loud enough, they can rewrite history and people will believe them. Look at Yasser Arafat."

Jeff said, "I've heard of him. He was a politician, right?"

Mary replied, "Not really. In 1996, he publicly stated that he planned to eliminate the state of Israel and that Arabs would then take over everything. That was his definition of 'peace.' He signed peace deals but then broke them. He took hundreds of millions of dollars from the U.S. that was meant to improve life for his people, but diverted the money for terrorist purposes. He kept lots for himself—he was filthy rich. President Clinton helped him along by refusing to hold him accountable. Arafat used every media platform he could get to preach hatred of Jews and sympathy for his people. Somehow his tactics worked because they actually awarded him a Nobel Peace Prize. Stupidity like that continues to this day. Look at how the Iranian president is now claiming the Holocaust never happened. Every book on the topic contradicts him and many survivors are still living, yet he still hopes enough lies will change things. When they're not attacking, they're practicing psychological warfare. They learned all this from the Nazis. They do it because people get intimidated and believe the lies when they hear them enough."

"So Ahmadinejad is next in line to get a Peace Prize?" Jeff joked.

Steve jumped in and said, "Israel's in a region that's mostly desert, although I've heard Israel has irrigated farmlands right up to the border, then it's just desert beyond the border. Maybe that's why the neighbors always want Israel's land. Plus Israelis are smart. They have democracy, technology, and good colleges and hospitals. One-third of all Nobel Prize winners are Israelis. With one-one thousandth of the world's population, they get one-third of the awards. It's amazing."

That was just a taste of what they had learned recently in preparation for their move to Israel. But Mary hadn't really answered Jeff's question about why Israel was persecuted. They were indeed God's chosen people and a blessed people, but for that reason, the Bible says Satan has pursued Israel to persecute it ever since the nation was born. The persecution included what the Romans did 2,000 years ago, then the Crusades, the Inquisition, and the Holocaust. It continues to this day. As though that wasn't scary enough, Steve, Mary and Jeff didn't realize what Iran and al-Qaeda were jointly preparing in retaliation for Israel's recent bombing of Iran.

THE BEGINNING OF THE END

The Van de Kamps arrived in Tel Aviv the next day after their overnight flight. They immediately noticed a larger presence of security at the airport than at any other airport they had been to. They gathered their belongings, and took a taxi to a hotel.

In the next week, things quickly fell into place for Steve and his family as they adapted to their new host country. The transition wasn't too hard. Israel was a lot like America, though there certainly were some differences. The architecture was different in some spots, the TV shows were different, the language was not strictly English, there was a different currency, grocery stores did not contain all the food that they were used to, and the list could go on. The world thought of it as the home of Judaism, but like in America, some people took their religion very seriously while some didn't.

There was one major difference. As Steve and Mary had explained to Jeff, here they were for the first time in their lives in that part of the world where history went back 2,000 years, to the time of Christ and even before that. Now they lived within 100 miles of where Jesus was born, lived, and died. This thought both excited and fascinated Steve. What would it feel like to see the exact spots where Jesus walked?

The day had come to find out. The family had gotten their household goods and car delivered after the ship arrived. Steve dropped off Mary at work one Friday morning and took off alone for Jerusalem. Jeff had decided to stay home and catch up with friends back home on the internet now that the computer had finally been unpacked and set up. Steve was nervous about his first drive of any real distance in the new country, but he had driven in England before on the left side of the road, so he thought he would be okay.

His car, average in size by American standards, seemed big on the narrow roads of Israel. In two slow hours, Steve covered the sixty miles and arrived in Jerusalem. The city was not a small, sleepy town like he envisioned. It had a population of about ¾ of a million people. Even 2,000 years ago, it was probably not a small or sleepy town; Bethlehem and Nazareth probably were, but Jerusalem has always been a big hub of activity. Steve followed the signs for "The Old City," the most famous and historic part of town where all the tourists went. Before long, he was there.

To his chagrin, Steve found out that no autos are allowed in the Old City. It was a fairly small area though so he would just have to find a place outside to park and then proceed on foot. He drove around a little to get his bearings and found a road that headed along the east side of the Old City, and he parked at what looked like a church. The moment was at hand. This was one of those days when Steve would finally get to see things that he'd heard about and seen pictures of all his life. He got out of the car and saw before him the best view of the Temple Mount, the Old City and the rest of Jerusalem he'd find anywhere.

Steve took in the view for awhile, and then went into the church he had parked in front of. He found out it was called the Chapel of Dominus Flevit. It was built in 1955 in the shape of a tear to commemorate the Lord's weeping over Jerusalem. The meaning of the Church's name was "The Cry of the Master." In this place, according to tradition, Christ cried when he got to Jerusalem. It was also where he predicted the destruction of the temple.

Steve also found out that he was on the Mount of Olives, and was near the Garden of Gethsemane, sites he wanted to see as much as any in Jerusalem. He threw on his backpack with his camera, guidebook and water bottle, shut the car door and set off on foot to explore what was around him. Steve walked to the Garden, that spot where Jesus spent his last night praying and then was approached by a crowd sent by the chief priests who took him into custody.

Steve wandered around deep in thought. Eventually he left the Garden and headed for the nearby highest part of the Mount of Olives. This had even more significance than the Garden. On this Mount, Jesus gave his Olivet Discourse. The Discourse was similar to the famous Sermon on the Mount, except this time the topic was the last days and the end of the age; how appropriate, since this happened just days before Jesus' death.

After His resurrection, Jesus rose to heaven from right there on the Mount of Olives. What Steve thought most deeply about though was that this is the spot, on all the earth, where he believed Jesus would return some day in the future. Steve looked up at the sky and wondered what things would look like on that day at that moment. He practically felt like Moses standing on sacred ground as he slowly walked around and pondered the history and the future of man. He remained deep in thought for quite some time.

Steve was glad he had come alone without his family. He had a way of being fascinated by history and thoughts of what had happened here. He could stroll around with a head full of such thoughts for far longer than most people would be interested. He wanted to take it all in, and he did so at his own speed.

Steve eventually left the area for the short walk to the Old City, his other destination of the day. Before long, there it was before him, the Western Wall, better known as the Wailing Wall. It looked bigger and older than he imagined, but still was just a wall that suddenly seemed overrated. What had all the fuss been about? He walked closer, and started to notice the other people nearby. There were Jewish people praying at the base of the wall. Suddenly, Steve heard someone yell, "You there!"

He looked over to where the voice came from. A policeman approached. "Great," Steve said to himself. "I've already broken some law I don't even know about."

The policeman knew a tourist when he saw one. He said, "Please observe the signs. Unless you're here to pray, you're required to stay back."

Steve was relieved to hear it was nothing more than that and he quickly complied. After backing up, he looked up and thought about the history of the place. He was at the base of the Temple Mount in Jerusalem, which represented the greatest point of sanctity for the Jewish people. On the hilltop at the top of the wall was where Abraham brought his son to be sacrificed. Centuries later, but still before the time of Christ, King Solomon built the temple there. It housed the Ark of the Covenant, which contained the Ten Commandments and the Torah, the Bible's first five books written by Moses. Jews were required to make a pilgrimage there three times a year. The temple was destroyed by the

Babylonians in 586 BC, but rebuilt in 515 BC. Centuries later, King Herod added to the rebuilt temple by making it much larger. Just a few years after completion though, it was torn down by Roman armies in 70 AD, thus fulfilling the prophetic words of Jesus that it would be destroyed. The site remained to this day the center and direction of Jewish prayer.

The spot was also sacred to Muslims because they claim it was from here that Mohammed began his ascent into Heaven. That was around 630 AD, after Muslims took over the city. Then they built the Dome of the Rock that stands on the hilltop to this day. Steve pulled out his guidebook and read a bit of recent history:

> "In 2002, a bulge appeared in the wall on its southern side. Archeologists determined it was caused by the construction of an underground mosque near the wall. Muslim officials made a vain attempt to repair the damage, and forbade Israeli officials from assisting. They warned that the wall's collapse is imminent. The bulge has increased in size since then. Should the wall collapse, the Arab world will undoubtedly blame Israel, despite its refusal to let Israelis help, and claim that it was due to Jewish efforts to destroy Islamic holy sites and rebuild Solomon's Temple. This could lead to regional warfare, and eventually engulf the world's 1.3 billion Muslims worldwide. The wall has therefore come to be referred to as the 'Armageddon Wall.'"

Steve looked for signs of the bulge, but couldn't see any. He took some photos, and then continued along. Steve enjoyed meandering along some of the streets and alleys of the Old City, a place that lives up to its name. Then he came upon one of the area's larger buildings, the Church of the Holy Sepulcher. Many people think it's the site of the death, burial, and resurrection of Jesus Christ. In the 4th century, Helena, the mother of Roman Emperor Constantine and a convert to Christianity, identified this as the location of the crucifixion. Her son then built a magnificent church on the spot. The church was destroyed and rebuilt several times over the centuries. The building Steve now gazed at dated from the 12th century.

Steve walked inside and admired the architecture. When he exited, he looked toward the east, the direction he had come from, and got a great view of the Temple Mount and its walls, the Dome of the Rock on top, and beyond that the Mount of Olives. It was all an area of such extraordinary history and importance.

Then suddenly, in the blink of an eye, came a bright light and a loud crash in the distance, like a huge crack of lightning and thunder. It came from the direction that Steve was looking. It was so loud that the ground shook and dropped Steve to his knees. He felt what seemed like a shock wave or sonic boom. He remained there on his hands and knees, shaking, and not sure what had happened. It was not an earthquake, since it had happened much too suddenly.

Moments later, Steve looked again in the same direction he had been looking, but now much of the city was blocked by a cloud of smoke and dust. It must have been a bomb, the kind they have seen so many of in this part of the world.

The sound dissipated quickly, but the dust and smoke remained. Steve now stood up and looked around. The city had changed in a few seconds, as though it had disappeared. The scene was now one of no noise; not a sound, not a car or siren, just silence. Most of the city was blocked from Steve's vantage point by the smoke. Steve didn't know what to do, so he just stood and looked and listened.

Before long, he heard a siren, and soon the streets were full of multiple sirens. It was 3:00 in the afternoon. The wind was blowing to the east so the smoke slowly started to drift away. As it did, Steve could see flashing lights in several locations. Steve had heard about people who were drawn to ground zero in New York City on 9–11. He felt that draw now. After waiting awhile, it was time to walk toward the sirens and find out what happened and see if he could help.

What Steve saw as he got closer to the blast site got worse and worse. Buildings were badly damaged. Many people were walking around dazed and in need of help. Many others were lying on the ground, unable to even get up. Steve heard a shout directed his way, "Hey you, come over here."

Steve looked and saw a paramedic who had yelled for his help. He went to him and asked what he needed.

"Take this roll of gauze and wrap up that man's arms," he was instructed. Steve started toward the man that lay nearby and looked for a moment before proceeding. The man's arms had been changed from flesh color to a terrible mixture of black and red; black from burns, red from blood. Steve then began wrapping his arms up to protect them. Apparently the man had been given morphine, that or he was in shock, because he sat there without showing much pain. Steve asked him his name.

He replied, "Mark."

"Do you know what happened?"

Steve got no reply, just a dazed look. When he finished the wraps, he went to the paramedic and asked him what had happened.

"Some kind of bomb," was the reply. "We've seen plenty of them around here over the years, but I haven't seen one this bad." Steve proceeded to help several people; washing wounds here, providing a needed drink there, even helping to immobilize some broken bones. Emergency lights still flashed everywhere but at least the sirens were turned off, probably to help everyone calm down, and to help communications too.

After two hours, Steve finally stopped to catch his breath. The smoke was gone, and he looked around. It finally dawned on him as he looked toward the wall that it had been damaged—badly damaged. Furthermore, the golden dome on the top above the wall, the top of the Dome of the Rock, was no longer visible. The dome and the rest of the building had been damaged or destroyed. Steve was new in this country and only knew a little of its long history and traditions, but he knew this would have a deep meaning. In fact, he recalled how just a couple hours ago he had read about the impact something like this would have.

Steve saw some news crews nearby. His last bad experience with a TV interview made him hope that none of them approached him. It did, however, make him think of Mary. He pulled out his cell phone and called her. To his surprise, he got through. She had been listening to the news, as had nearly everybody in the country by now. "Steve," she said, "I've been trying to call and worried about you. Are you alright?"

"Yeah, I'm okay," he responded. "It was close though. I was right here in Jerusalem when it happened. I'm fine. I think I was just far enough away to not get hurt. What are they saying about it on the news?"

Mary said, "Mostly they're just trying to count up the dead and injured and describing the part of the city where it happened. They said there are at least 100 dead, and many injured. Are you going to be able to make it home?" she asked.

"It might take a while, but I can make it," he replied. It was just then that it dawned on him that the damage seemed to have gotten worse the closer he got to the spot where his car was. "Mary, I think our car got damaged. I don't know yet, I haven't gotten to it to see. I better head that way and find out."

"Oh Steve, our only car," Mary uttered, but then realized things could be much worse. Suddenly, she heard a shout over the phone from Steve's end, and then the phone connection went dead.

"Hold it; back up," Steve heard get shouted his way as he walked along. Steve looked over and saw the policeman who had just shouted at him.

"What's wrong?" he replied.

"Back up," he repeated. "Get away from the danger zone. We're going to rope off this whole area. You can't go in there. Everything's damaged too badly, we need it for evidence, and there may be radiation too."

"What do you mean radiation?" Steve asked.

"The bomb may have been a radiation bomb, you know, a suitcase bomb. A small nuclear bomb, and that would give off radiation. We must back up."

"But," Steve yelled, "My car is somewhere up ahead."

"Trust me, you won't be getting it anytime soon," the policeman responded. "We have to go get showered off."

For a moment, Steve wondered how he would get home, but then he realized he had bigger problems than that. He walked with the policeman to a mobile shower facility that had been set up. They were instructed to strip and put their clothes in a bag that was handed to them. He showered and was given some different clothes to wear afterwards. Steve then found an emergency worker and asked what he should do. He was escorted into another tent and given some medicine to drink, some iodine something-or-other is all Steve could remember of its name. He was then told that he may as well go home and listen to the news about what people who had been in this area should do in terms of follow-up medical care. Steve felt fine, but the issue for him was possible exposure to radiation, and if so, how much had there been.

The buses weren't running anywhere near that part of town. Later, Steve managed to find an officer with a car who drove him to the main bus terminal where Steve was able to take a bus back to Tel Aviv. He got to Tel Aviv around 11:00 that night. Mary, who had been eventually able to reach Steve again by phone, had borrowed a neighbor's car and met him at the bus terminal. They saw each other and embraced. When they got home, Jeff was watching the news. He gave his dad a hug. Steve was tired but too worked up to sleep. The three watched news coverage and talked long into the night.

The next morning was more of the same. They all hoped the reporters would know more of what had happened by now. It didn't take long to find out that that was the case. Shortly after turning on the TV, they heard that the death toll was over 300, plus at least 1,000 that were hospitalized. *Yes*, Steve thought to himself, *a little worse timing, and things could have been a lot worse for me.*

The news continued. Various reporters were referring to the explosion as everything from a suitcase bomb to a backpack bomb. It apparently was not a "dirty bomb" where some explosive like TNT gets surrounded by radioactive material to disperse the radiation. That causes relatively minor physical damage, but the radiation can cause great psychological damage.

This was, instead, an actual nuclear device. It was small and had nowhere the power of a large atomic bomb, but still was a nuclear bomb that delivered the explosive power of about 100 tons of TNT. That's enough to do great physical damage, and the attackers had indeed been successful in that respect. Radiation was also released, and that had Steve worried. He watched the news as they showed coverage from near the blast zone, which was on the side of the Mount of Olives. They discussed the high possibility of many square blocks having to be closed off for weeks or months while they took measures to make it safe again for habitation and reconstruction. As they showed maps on the TV screen of this area, Steve realized his car had been in a spot very close to the center of the area being closed.

The phone rang and Mary answered it. "Steve," she said, "it's for you," and she handed the phone to Steve.

"Steve Van de Kamp?" someone inquired.

"Speaking," Steve replied.

He hung up a minute later and said to Mary, "That was someone from Jerusalem. They said I should go to a hospital today and get tested for radiation."

Coincidentally, they lived just a few blocks from a hospital. Steve felt fine so he walked to the hospital by himself. When he got home a couple hours later, Mary and Jeff were anxious as he walked in.

"Steve, what did you find out?" Mary asked.

Steve explained to her, "Apparently I got lucky. I did have a slightly high level of radiation in me, but no worse than what most smokers have. I never got closer than about half of a mile from the blast, just far enough away that my exposure was minimal. On top of that, the wind was blowing the right way for my sake. Walking back toward the blast afterwards wasn't the smartest thing for me to do in retrospect, but still, how could I have known?" They talked for awhile, and then Steve took a nap.

Later, the family sat down for dinner. "Anything new on the news?" Steve asked.

Jeff answered, "Not much, but I found out that these suitcase and backpack bombs have been around for years. They come in different sizes and pack different loads of power. It looks like this one was small. They're also naming a few terrorist groups that may have done it."

"Small, but still, look at all the damage it did," Mary was quick to point out.

"So they finally did it," Steve chimed in. "They finally got themselves a nuclear bomb, and they used it, too. Maybe we should say a prayer." They prayed as Steve, Mary and Jeff all asked God for help with this situation. This was not what they had envisioned life to be like in Israel, and they had only been there a week and a half.

After the prayer and during dinner, Jeff asked his dad, "Why do we pray? Does it do any good? I mean, look what happened."

"I know what you mean," Steve answered. "That's why we have a bad habit of only praying when there's an emergency like now, or after 9–11, or when miners get trapped in a cave. God tells us to pray though. He doesn't say all our prayers will be answered the way we want, but he asks us to pray for his will to be done." He paused for a moment, then added, "Everything that happens is either what God wants, or at least what He let's happen. He has reasons, and He knows far more than we do. Sometimes it might take years for us to see the big picture. For example, look at the 1990's. Maybe God let Bill Clinton get elected president because he knew Clinton would ignore terrorism. That led to 9–11, and that led to Bush going into Iraq. Without Clinton and 9–11, that never happens, and maybe God was ready for some change in the Middle East."

"Just like in Europe in the 1930's and 40's," Mary added. "The Holocaust was awful—six million Jews murdered. But without it, Israel probably would never have been reinstated as a nation in 1948 like it was."

"What do you mean? How are they related?" Jeff asked.

Mary replied, "The world basically felt sorry for what had happened to the Jews because they had been horribly wronged. To make it up to them, the United Nations voted to give them back their country just after World War II in 1948. Israel actually didn't exist with any borders anywhere for around 2,500 years before that. Without the Holocaust, that would probably never have happened. In fact, there was only a short window for it to happen in 1948 because many nations have hated Israel and done all they could to destroy it ever since, and that includes the UN. The return of Israel and many of its people is even prophesized in the Bible, and sure enough, it happened. It was painful; six million deaths was probably not the answer to anybody's prayers, except maybe Hitler's, but it was God's path to progress."

Then Steve added, practically with a laugh, "Like they say, God never watches world events and says wow, I didn't see that coming and I blew it." Steve paused and then added, "I've heard people, including famous political analysts, say if Hillary wins the upcoming presidential election, they will move out of the U.S. That shows they just don't get it. If she wins, it's what God wants. It doesn't necessarily mean she's the best candidate; it means that's who God wants there or allows to be there for some reason at that point in time."

"Maybe the winner really is the best candidate," Jeff interceded.

"Usually," Steve replied, "but you never know. Again, look at history. Have you ever heard of Ross Perot?"

"No, who's he?"

"He's a business man who ran for president in 1992 with a third party. He got 20% of the vote; not nearly enough to win, but a huge number of votes that were mostly taken away from President Bush. Without Perot, Bush probably wins by a comfortable margin. So from out of nowhere, this guy appeared and had a rather miraculous impact on the outcome of the election. Clinton became president and it changed the future of the world like I just said."

They ate for a while, then something crossed Steve's mind, "I wonder if our auto insurance covers us against suicide bombers?"

"I'll bet there's some fine print escape clause titled 'suicide bombers,'" Mary quipped.

Steve said, "Maybe we can find one of those famous Jewish lawyers who can get it labeled as jihad instead. I can hear it now in court. Sir, could you explain why your car is now totaled?"

Mary quickly responded with, "That depends on what the definition of 'is' is." They all got a big laugh out of that one. It was many moments like this when Steve reminded himself of how lucky he was with having found Mary again. She could tell a joke better than anyone.

Everybody had a lot to think about during the rest of dinner that night and in the days to come. The final death tally climbed to 419. The number was held down due to the explosion happening in a parking lot just outside of town with few people in the immediate area.

In the news, along with the number of dead was the

future of the Temple Mount wall and what gets built on the top. Maybe more importantly was the verbal fight breaking out over who controlled the land and who would repair and rebuild it. Not surprisingly, the Israelis had one idea; the Arabs had another. This was nothing new, but now they had something new to fight about. As for who was responsible, all that was being said by the police was that investigative work was on-going, they had leads, and progress was being made.

Two days later, there was a knock at the door of Steve and Mary. Steve answered the door. It was the police. The head officer inquired, "Are you Steven Van de Kamp?"

Steve replied, "Yes."

"You're under arrest for suspicion in the Jerusalem bombing." Steve was handcuffed and put in a police car for a drive to the police station.

Who's to Blame?

It was an intense ride to the police station, although nothing was said by anyone on the way. The police had many questions for Steve, and he had many of his own for them. He wondered what could have led to this, and if there would be a sea of news reporters at the police station. There certainly would be if word had gotten out about an arrest, and in fact, that was the case. At the station, Steve was quickly hustled out of the car and through a noisy crowd, and then led into a building where he was confronted by the man who seemed to be in charge. He said his name was Inspector Erving. He had Steve take a seat.

The Inspector seemed stern but fair as he spoke, "Do you know why you have been brought here?"

"No," Steve replied. "I've only been told that somehow you think I'm connected to the Jerusalem bombing."

"Yes, you are deeply involved," the Inspector said. "The bomb that went off was in your car. Enough scraps of metal were pieced together for us to be sure of that. The question is why did you do this?

"You're wrong," Steve shot back. "I know nothing about this. I'm no terrorist. I'm no bomb expert. I did nothing.

Maybe the bomb went off near my car. The explosion happened a couple hours after I parked my car and left it. Maybe somebody even stuck the bomb under my car and used the car to hide it."

The inspector had enormous pressure on him to provide answers. He was assigned to this case because he was experienced. He had worked day and night since the explosion and had done his homework. He thought and then said, "Mr. Van de Kamp, we've looked into your background. You are an electronics and engineering expert. You just came to this country. The bomb went off in your car, not underneath it. There is no doubt of that. But you are right. There are many things about this that don't seem to suggest you would do such a thing. But someone did, and you're the only suspect we have. I'm looking for answers. What can you tell me?"

"Plenty," Steve said. "Check my records if you haven't already. I've never worked in munitions. I know nothing about bombs. I have nothing against Israel. I've got no criminal record. It's not like I snuck into the country. I'm here because my wife got transferred to the U.S. Embassy."

"Yes, we've checked out all that," the Inspector said. "You're under suspicion, but I have my doubts about your implication. It doesn't add up. Your car was transferred here by ship, correct?"

"Yes. It was out of our possession for three weeks."

"I have men looking into that, and maybe that will tell us something." Inspector Erving looked out the window. "You saw the crowd out there that this matter has generated. There is pressure to get answers quickly, but of course we also have to get the right answers. Since you are an American citizen who came here recently, the American government is looking into this along with our own officials. The media will undoubtedly do all the poking they can also. Your name and face will be all over the place soon if it's not already. In fact, part of my job is to announce what we know about you."

Steve asked, "What now? I need to get a lawyer and get bailed out of here."

The Inspector warned him though, "Mr. Van de Kamp, get a lawyer, but forget about leaving here. Four hundred and nineteen people are dead. A city is partly in ruins. One or more people somewhere are responsible. It might be you. There will not be any chance for bail at this point. You don't want to leave here anyway. You might be killed if you left, plus you need to keep yourself away from the media. Surely you've seen the news and seen the anger there is over this. Some people are ready for blood at the first sign of responsibility for this bombing, and they're not in a mood to wait for much proof. You're far better off here in custody than anywhere."

Steve hadn't really had a chance to collect his thoughts until then, but that made sense to him, not that he had a choice.

Like the Inspector had said, Steve's face was suddenly all over the Israeli news that day. Steve's quick walk by the cameras on the way into the police station had been enough to enable and ensure that. 9–11 had resulted in non-stop news coverage on every television news channel in the United States for three days, and this story was just as large in this part of the world.

Back at home, Mary hadn't been able to reach Steve by phone since he was taken away. She had seen Steve leave, but the first thing she learned after that was what she saw about Steve on TV. Very shortly after that, the police arrived at her house again. This time she was taken to the same police station. She wanted to see Steve and was told that would happen soon, but only after some questioning. Even though the vehicle was also hers, the police saw nothing in her background to suggest she was implicated.

Eventually the police let Mary see Steve. She was glad to see him, but was scared and confused about these circumstances. "Steve, what's going on?" were her first words to him.

By now, Steve had been talked to twice more by Inspector Erving and others. He had calmed down and tried to calm Mary as well. "I don't really know," he began, "but everything will be alright. I was in the wrong place at the wrong time, but I think they know I did nothing. Unless they're looking for a scapegoat, things will be okay eventually and I'll get out of here."

Mary said fearfully, "You should see the crowd outside. It's like a lynch mob. They want a scapegoat."

Again Steve calmed her, "This is a civilized country. The crowd might be unruly, but nothing crazy is going to happen. I'll be fine. The problem will be sneaking you out of here."

Steve Van de Kamp's life and history were suddenly being thoroughly reviewed as the investigators combed over U.S. federal, state and local records about him, plus information they had gathered from Mary, and what they found at Steve and Mary's house after a visit with a search warrant. He was quickly getting as much scrutiny as a presidential candidate. Steve's past was coming into focus for the entire world to see; one of those instances where the dots were there but nobody connected them until it was too late. Here's what they realized:

Steve had been forced into retirement by the U.S. military

This led to his divorce

The divorce court ripped most of what he had worked his whole life for away from him

Finally, he again served his country admirably in the Missile Defense Program, only to be forced out again.

When all this came to light, it appeared that maybe Steve had reached the breaking point, sought revenge, and found an enormous way to do so. Israel was talking about little else these days except how to rebuild and who to blame, and Steve was their man for the blame part.

Mary visited Steve again at the police station and informed him that this was happening. "Steve, they say the bomb was inside the vehicle, not underneath it. Any finger prints of other people that may have been on the bomb got burned off. I know you're innocent, but they don't."

Steve was worried, but responded, "They're ignoring one fact: they have no motive. If I was mad at the U.S., why would I blow up a bomb over here?"

The Israeli police realized they still had some nagging questions like that one so they kept open minds and kept looking for evidence and answers.

Two days later, Inspector Erving met again with Steve early in the morning. Steve was ready for more bad news, but that did not happen. Instead, the inspector said, "The case is not solved, but we now know that you were not the perpetrator."

"What?" Steve asked. "What did you say?"

"We got a tip from someone," the inspector explained. It led to us discovering that your vehicle was broken into during its transport here on the ship and the bomb was placed in it at that time. You've been driving a rolling bomb ever since."

Steve was processing all this. "I never saw anything. I never heard anything. Where was it?"

The Inspector answered, "They don't call it a suitcase bomb for nothing. It's small; suitcase sized. They removed your spare tire and put it there. Here's the interesting part. They also put a GPS tracker with it so they could follow your vehicle's every move. They knew right where you were so they could detonate it when they wanted, presumably when the vehicle was where they could do maximum damage. It wasn't on a timer. They could detonate it anytime they threw a remote switch."

"Who's they?" Steve asked. "Do you know who did it?"

"We think it's a band of terrorists from Hezbollah. We have two suspects." He showed Steve photos of two men. "Do you know either of these men?"

Steve looked and thought. "I know one of them...from somewhere." He thought some more. "I've seen him," pointing at one. "I think I met him a month or two ago, back in the U.S. He was a cameraman for a Los Angeles TV station. I forget his name though."

Steve was right—it was the same person he had met at Vandenburg AFB; a man who apparently had successfully obtained that job as a cover, and maybe as a way to obtain information. Had he somehow followed the demise of Steve's career after that interview in California? Had Steve's background and his move overseas made him just the right person for someone to frame?

Steve continued to talk with the inspector and others in the room. "I guess their whole plot depended on me not getting a flat tire and seeing the bomb. Why would these terrorists pick the location they did for detonation? I assume they're Muslims. They blew up their own shrine, the Dome of the Rock. That makes no sense to me."

"We cannot say anything more at this time," Steve was told. "We will take you home now. We'll contact you as needed."

Steve was driven to his home in Tel Aviv and was told to stay there. A guard was posted outside at the house he and Mary had rented since their arrival in the country.

This major terrorist incident was receiving attention at the highest levels. Several phone calls had occurred between President George Bush and Israeli Prime Minister Ehud Olmert, the man who replaced Ariel Sharon. Many other conversations also occurred between various Cabinet members of the two countries. With each day, the political situation in Israel got more complicated for Mr. Olmert, due to the nature of the city of Jerusalem. All three of the world's major religions, Christianity, Judaism, and Islam, have a major presence in Jerusalem. Jerusalem is the religious capital of the world, but that has never made it a city of peace. It had always made for a volatile mix instead. For example, Muslims had recently banned all non-Muslims from the Temple Mount and destroyed many Jewish structures and replaced them with mosques. Some thought this was a master plan by Yasser Arafat to remove all traces of Jewish history at the site and transform it into an Islam complex to rival others such as Mecca. Conversely, Ariel Sharon and now Olmert had pledged to prevent that from happening and to reopen the Temple Mount to Jews.

As usual, Israel just wanted to peacefully co-exist with its neighbors, whereas the Arab world wanted to wipe out Israel, Jews and their history. Sharon was now gone, but his successor had inherited all the same problems.

Later that day, Prime Minister Olmert summoned Inspector Erving and his staff to his office to get a briefing on recent developments. The Inspector arrived and told the Minister and his staff what he had found out from Steve about the suspect they had the photo of.

The minister then changed the tone of the meeting by addressing everyone and saying, "Gentlemen, as you know, the war of words is quickly escalating as to who will control the rebuilding of the Temple Mount. Violence is threatening to break out in the city between the two sides. We need answers to prevent this, and we need them fast. What do we know?"

"Our theory about the bombing," someone explained, "is that they had much more in mind than just doing some physical damage. They were making a political statement, and exacting revenge."

"Revenge for what?"

"Revenge for our bombing of Iran a month ago. Iran has wanted to retaliate against us ever since, and it looks like they got Hezbollah to do it for them. For the same reason we couldn't do more than a one day bombing run against them, they also had limited options against us. This may have been their best option. They hoped this bomb would enable someone else to take the blame—the American. That was their hope. Now we know it wasn't him but a terrorist arm, but unfortunately we still cannot place blame squarely on Iran."

Someone else said, "Look at recent history. In 2005, the U.S. got us to withdraw from Gaza and we lost the land. In 2006, we fought Lebanon and the U.S. stood by watching and even wanted us to give up. Now this blast that we were blaming the U.S. for. The real enemy is driving a wedge between us and the West. That was their intention, and it's working."

Then Minister Olmert spoke and said, "Most of all, look at how the blast has united the Arab world. Besides fighting us, they have also fought each other for decades; Iraq against Kuwait, Iran against Iraq, on and on. But now, the whole Arab world is suddenly united with each other, and against us. It is a grave situation. No wonder they were willing to destroy their own holy site to accomplish this. They have other more prominent sites, so their Dome of the Rock was a small enough price to pay for this outcome." He paused and then said, "What do we do now?"

"Sir," his deputy spoke up and said. "We have been preparing to defend ourselves again since our battle ended with Lebanon in 2006. We all knew that cease fire was most likely just temporary. Once we know for sure who sponsored this attack, we must retaliate against them, whether it's Iran, Lebanon, or Syria. I recommend you order preparations for such an effort."

"I agree," the Minister said. To his staff he added, "We will convene daily to discuss the status of this matter."

After some further discussion, the meeting was over. The course of action had been decided upon. Given the conditions though, it had been little more than a formality. A chain of events had once again forced this small, unique nation into a course of military action that it did not want, but had to accept.

Back at the Van de Kamps' home, things were far from normal. Things had never yet been normal since their still recent arrival in this new country. The breaking news about Steve's innocence had now made its way over the airwaves. Steve and Mary worried if people would believe this recent turn of events or if people would think America strong-armed Israel into some politically acceptable alternative story.

After Steve's return home from the police station, he and Mary wondered what would happen next. Jeff joined them at the kitchen table. "Dad, what's going to happen now? Are we going to have to go back home?"

"That might happen eventually, but for now they're telling us we can't go anywhere," Steve replied. "I barely know what's ahead though. They seemed to be ramping up for war at the police station this morning. Israel had trouble last year just trying to beat Lebanon. What if they now connect the attack with Syria or Iran? That's almost sure to happen and may lead to large scale war."

"The U.S. will apply their normal double standard," Mary said. "We have a strict policy of not negotiating with terrorists, but we expect Israel to sit around and do nothing but negotiate. That means giving away more land and doing whatever else it takes to maintain the peace, so maybe there won't be a war."

"The old rules might not apply anymore," Steve added. "We've entered a new age. We're back to using nukes. People are scared, people are mad and people are ready for action, just like back home after 9–11."

"Maybe it was Russia that provided the bomb," Jeff said. "Aren't Iran and other countries still trying to go nuclear but not there yet?"

Mary had researched this very subject and said, "Right, but any country could have bought a bomb from Russia. It's reported that Russia still has 16,000 nukes. From what I hear, they've done a terrible job of managing them. They admit they don't know where many of them are. The U.S. tried to talk to Moscow about this back in 2002 but talks fizzled out. Many are missing or have been stolen, and some could have been sold. Russia has needed money for years and these oil countries have money. Iran and Russia have been cooperating with each other for years. There are many reports saying nukes have changed hands."

"Then there's Saudi Arabia," Steve said. "They seem to always get what they want. That's where the most influential Islam schools are and that's why most hijackers on 9–11 were from Saudi Arabia, yet look how we went into Afghanistan and Iraq instead. Saudi Arabia always get a free pass; another Washington double standard. We buy far more oil from Saudi than from any other country so they get a free pass, probably because they're willing to trade using U.S. dollars. On top of that, they bought off Washington,

D.C. Israel seems to get blamed for all the wars. Nut jobs even claim Jews knew 9–11 was coming and got out in time, although they never provide a shred of evidence. The Saudi's bought the State Department and half of the rest of Washington which enables them to start stories like that one and blame Israel for everything. They also lobby the UN to blame Israel, and they've been tremendously successful."

Mary chimed in, "They still practice beheadings in that country. They don't allow Jews in their country. They actually accomplished what Hitler dreamed of—a Jew-free society."

Then Steve added, "You know, maybe that's why we never drill for more oil in Alaska. The Alaska pipeline from the 70's proved that we could drill and transport oil there with no ecological disturbance, yet here we are with the tree-hugging laws to prevent more drilling. Alaska has enough reserves to make us oil independent, but we refuse to do it. They claim we have to protect the caribou. In a nation that legalizes abortion, a nation that doesn't mind murdering 40 million of our own babies, we supposedly care about some caribou that none of us ever see. Maybe Saudi Arabia bought out Congress and the lobbyists and successfully got us to undermine ourselves to keep paying them oil money to make the rich Saudis even richer."

Mary was on a roll and said, "The Saudi Embassy in Washington has repeatedly told the U.S. that they're not funding terrorist groups, but it's been proven that they fund al-Qaeda, Hamas, Hezbollah and others. Their Ambassador to the U.S. owns a $150 million house in Aspen, and that's just his vacation home. When they're not funding terrorists and bribing us, they're just buying us up. They're building mosques in the U.S. too. Many mosques are training centers where terrorism is preached and weapons are hidden. Some experts say they have small nukes stored in some of them, but judges won't give law enforcement a warrant to investigate."

"Some day...," Steve thought, almost trembling. "Some day one or more nukes are going to go off in the U.S. Then people are going to panic, and cry, and wonder how it happened. Then we will waste so much time pointing fingers all over again."

Even Jeff with his high school education displayed more common sense than all of the White House and Congress combined when he said, "The president could have helped his oil buddies and made the country stronger and decreased our energy independence all with one simple decision to drill in Alaska. Instead, we strengthened our enemies, hurt our ally Israel, run massive deficits, weaken the dollar, fight a war, and have 40 thousand soldiers dead or injured in Iraq—it makes no sense! We could have avoided all this by not making the Middle East rich with oil revenue which enables them to live out their crazy fantasies."

President Bush had called Islam a religion of peace, but apparently he hadn't read the newspapers. Was he that naive? Was he purposely misleading his own countrymen in order to try to appease Muslims and not add to the potential for hostilities? Maybe it was the latter. Maybe the less Americans knew about this topic, the better. Americans knew very little about Muslims before 9–11. Afterwards, things didn't get much better, especially when the American president did his best to keep people in the dark. There was nothing wrong with hope and reaching out, but those things had been tried for years by former President Clinton and many others, but they still didn't prevent 9–11. In fact, history had proven over and over that appeasement didn't work. Britain and France appeasing Hitler didn't work. Appeasing Arafat made him the world's biggest terrorist. Appeasement only emboldened the enemy. Bush's Road Map to Peace was yet another attempt at appeasement that wasn't working—terrorists turned acquired land into terrorism headquarters.

There wasn't one example in history of Islam bringing peace anywhere it spread. The method used by Islam throughout history had been to convert foreigners or else enslave them or kill them. That was why only force worked on them. The irony of Islam even being called a "religion" never seemed to get through to people.

There was much more irony, or maybe "unexplainable" was a better term:

Suicide bombers were convinced to blow themselves up to go to their heaven where virgins await them. They hate the West for what they call a decadent, twisted, selfish, wasteful, materialistic lifestyle, yet Muslims sought a heavenly paradise full of everything they condemned the West for, such as unlimited sexual pleasure and wine (and they never explain where the virgins come from or why their leaders never blew themselves up).

Muslims down through history never wanted the land that Israel currently possessed until Israelis returned to their homeland in the later half of the 20th century and turned its deserts and swamps into fertile farmland.

Muslims claim that Jerusalem was one of their sacred religious centers, yet the Quran never mentions Jerusalem so their claim has no merit. Compare that to Christians and Jews, whose Bible mentions Jerusalem over 800 times and thereby clearly established its importance to those religions.

Arabs claimed to be the descendents of ancient Palestinians, but this was another recent attempt to change history and steal this title from Jews. The Quran also never mentioned the word "Palestine."

Steve, Mary and Jeff were right that all these obvious problems had been mishandled for years in America concerning the Middle East, as had many of the lessons from 9–11. Little did they know how that gross negligence would lead to all these problems soon becoming much worse.

The World Gets Involved

While the Middle East was in turmoil and unsure of what was ahead, Russia was working on plans of its own. Many Russian leaders had never been willing to accept Russia's diminished status since their loss in the Cold War. They sought a return for their nation to glory and world prominence. It is a huge nation with many natural resources, and an economy and technology that has been improving for years. Russia is the world's largest producer of natural gas and the second largest producer of oil. Natural gas is a commodity that is used more and more as a clean, efficient alternative to coal and other sources for such necessities as heating.

Russia's president, Vladimir Putin, was much more of a hard-liner from the old days of Russia than his two predecessors before him. Starting in the 1990's, Putin had decided to use natural gas, Russia's largest export, as the cornerstone of a plan to return his country to glory. Russia had spent years successfully building a huge natural gas pipeline distribution system. Gazprom is the name of Russia's state-owned gas monopoly that built this system. The system controlled the flow of gas from Russia to most European countries.

Russia profited greatly from natural gas sales since

this source of heat had become the commodity of choice in Europe and much of Asia. For years, the Russian government forced all Russian gas producers to sell their gas to Gazprom. Of course, this meant not just great profits for Russia, but also great power for Russia. Just like Saudi Arabia has great power and leverage due to its oil revenue, Russia had come to benefit greatly from its gas monopoly.

Europe feared this dependence upon Russia, but could not build its own pipeline until the year 2011 at the earliest. Of course, where Europe would obtain gas to pump through its own pipeline in the future was also a big question because Europe produced very little natural gas and very few countries exported it. Iran has the world's second largest reserves of natural gas, but Iran sells much of its supply to Russia. In fact, the two countries developed a natural gas cartel; like OPEC but for natural gas. This was an inevitable event since Russia is a much stronger ally with Iran than it is with European countries.

Europe had hoped this situation and its weakening ties with Russia might improve due to Russia's upcoming 2008 presidential election. Putin had served his maximum number of terms and couldn't run again. Unfortunately for Europe though, Putin was quite popular and that enabled him to virtually hand-pick his successor. Not surprisingly, the successor also did not embrace competition or European relations. He would prove to be no different than Putin.

Europe could now only hope that Russia did not try to take further advantage of the monopolistic power it possessed as the supplier of natural gas to Europe. On-going Russian-Iranian cooperation involving the exchange of oil, gas and arms was fueling an already explosive world situation.

The Jerusalem bombing and other recent world events had done their intended job and damaged relations between Israel and the United States. This was not remedied after the real source of the bomb, Hezbollah, had been discovered, partly due to the fact that the men involved were in hiding and were not captured. Furthermore, the Arab world had rallied together in an unprecedented manner as a result of the bombing. Never before had all the nations of the Middle East been united like this against Israel. Iran had planned and hoped for this as a result of the bombing, and was now planning the best way to capitalize on this situation moving forward. Their larger plan was still to annihilate Israel, and this worst case scenario looked like it was falling into place with the aid of the Arab world unification.

Iran had led the way in the Middle East for years toward this goal. They had provided the U.S. with dubious intelligence data concerning Saddam Hussein and Iraq several years earlier which had helped coerce the U.S. into his overthrow. Since then, Iran had also taken the lead in supplying the forces and equipment to insurgents in Iraq that had kept the U.S. in the quagmire there that they had been in for years. Iran was aided by their purchase of Russian technology and equipment which had been going on for years. The two nations had developed an extensive network of cooperation and contracts whereby each was getting from the other exactly what they sought. Russia had more military weapons than it knew what to do with, and Iran, like Saudi Arabia, had great wealth from its oil and gas revenue to buy the weapons.

Iran was also benefiting from the U.S. being too busy in Iraq to do anything about what Iran was doing or threatening to do. Iran was well aware of the problems the U.S. also had back home as the two American political parties put all their effort and attention into fighting with each other over how to proceed in Iraq, as well as how to win elections. This jawboning had ratcheted to a new high due to the upcoming 2008 presidential election. The United Nations similarly did some jawboning but did not have the will or forces to do anything about the Middle East situation.

After decades of not even being able to deal successfully with Iraq, Iran was now in the driver's seat in the Middle East as a result of all these events that they orchestrated with great political astuteness.

Iran had bought the suitcase bomb that was used in Jerusalem from Russia. They had also bought five more that they were ready to use. Their military and political leaders were contemplating whether they should try using them against Israel, or attack Israel with conventional forces. Iran had the army, equipment and momentum they needed for either; it was only a matter of time before they decided how to proceed and when.

The world had become an ever more dangerous place. The Bible calls Satan the "prince of this world" (John 12:31 and 14:30) and "the god of this age and world" (2 Corinthians 4:4). This is because he has been allowed to roam the world with great authority and power, especially the power of deception. He uses all this to scheme and set traps for us. His first trap was for Adam and Eve, and we humans fell for it just as he planned. He is the originator and the master of lies; he is the father of lies (John 8:44). He has spent all of human history leading the world astray and deceiving the nations (Revelation 12:9 and 20:3). He prowls around the earth like a roaring lion looking for someone to devour (1 Peter 5:8). He is still at it.

Satan wants Israel destroyed even more than the nations that publicly state they want Israel destroyed. While he is still here on earth, he needs to destroy Israel and all Jews to prevent his destiny in hell. This is because God promised to preserve the Jews and their nation of Israel since this is where Christ will return to reign over his people from his temple throne in Jerusalem. It is at Armageddon in Israel where Christ will save Israel and some of its people by defeating Satan and throwing him into hell forever. If Israel and Jews no longer exist, this cannot happen and God will be proven a liar and have no ground to judge or punish Satan or his antichrist. The world could then remain under Satan's control for eternity.

God called himself "the God of Israel" over 200 times because Israel is the key to the future of the world. The Bible mentions "Israel" over 2,500 times for a similarly good reason. Seventy percent of its contents cover Israel's history and prophesy her future. No wonder Satan has been posturing people, countries and events throughout history toward his objective of annihilating Israel. Pharaoh and Hitler were two of his most famous servants in this endeavor, and it continues right up to this day. His moment seems to be coming; in fact, it seems to be at hand.

Israel and Iran were on the verge of full-scale war with each other. Israel felt they were forced into this by the Jerusalem bombing. Prime Minister Olmert had the backing of his Cabinet to go to war, and so he notified his nation's military to be on high alert and prepare for war.

Iran was also prepared for war. It had been weighing its options concerning how best to capitalize on its sudden power in the region, unity in the Muslim world, and the lack of will by any foreign nations to stop it. Iran's leadership carefully considered what it felt were its two options:

1. Attempt to get its five suitcase nuclear devices into Israel and set them off at strategic locations, or

2. Launch a massive air and ground assault against Israel.

Each option had a potentially huge problem though for Iran. Hitting Israel with their five nukes could do much damage, but these five bombs were not nearly large enough to blow up the entire country or ensure an easy victory. In fact, detonation of these bombs would ensure that Israel would retaliate with their most powerful weapon—its arsenal of approximately 200 nuclear weapons. Thanks to Israeli scientists, Israel has had these for years. They are the largest variety, about 300 kilotons each, not the much smaller suitcase types that Iran had.

Conversely, if Iran proceeded with a conventional ground and air assault, they feared Israel would also resort to use of their nuclear weapons if Israel was not faring well in a war. Due to the recent use of a nuclear weapon in Jerusalem, even though it was a small device, the world had changed. The world had re-entered a nuclear age. Use of nuclear weapons was now less of a remote threat and much more likely. Iran had a history of throwing caution to the wind, but knew it had to proceed carefully in light of this.

A new player was entering the world political stage, right at this critical point in history when such a figure was needed. Ricardo Valentine had grown up in Italy where he had risen quickly through political positions in that country and also become a foreign diplomat. More recently, he had become the Deputy of the Secretary General of the United Nations. After a short time in that capacity, the Secretary General unexpectedly had health problems and resigned, and Mr. Valentine was promoted to the top UN position to replace him and became the Secretary General. He instantly faced great challenges in this high position.

The United Nations had been humiliated by the food for oil scandal a few years earlier. They had brokered that arrangement whereby Iraqi oil would be sold and the revenue would supposedly be used by Iraq to improve life for its citizens through the purchase of food and medicine. Saddam Hussein had instead used the money to build more palaces for himself, plus strengthen his military and terrorist network. This was going on with the UN's knowledge, but they stood by and did nothing about it. In fact, many members of the UN, including the son of the Secretary General at that time, actually profited greatly from this. Hussein was also paying off some UN members from France and Russia for their votes.

What was still much less known by the public was the UN's long-standing record of anti-Semitism. For example, numerous times the UN had condemned Israel for its military action when all Israel did was to defend itself after being attacked. The UN never condemned Israel's attackers. Over the years, Israel actually gave back about 95% of the land it captured in wars after it was attacked. This extraordinary gesture of peace is unprecedented in world history, yet the UN always treated Israel with disdain.

The last anti-Arab vote by the UN was in 1947. The UN never sided with Israel after Israel was formed in 1948. Numerous times the UN pressured Israel to give in to never-ending Arab demands for Israel to give away more land. It did nothing about Arab threats to annihilate Israel.

The Arab attacks were never just to challenge borders or gain ground, but to annihilate Israel altogether. No Arab or Muslim map even shows Israel on it.

The UN did nothing about terrorism in general. It ignored human rights violations. It had never allowed Israel to have membership on its Security Council, but it let terrorist states like Libya do so. It always welcomed Yasser Arafat and gave him standing ovations when he spoke. The UN mastered the arts of anti-Semitism and appeasement. What's more, the United Nations had never been condemned itself for its long record of damaging Israel.

The UN also had a long-standing bias against America. For example, in 1999, the UN General Assembly passed a Resolution aimed at pressuring the U.S. to abandon its plans to build its anti-missile defense system—the UN didn't mind terrorist activities but didn't want the U.S. to have defensive systems! Recent remarks by the American president about these matters had also hurt the UN's image.

The UN sought to repair its reputation after all this. It also sought a return to a more prominent world leadership role. It saw the current escalation of hostilities in the Middle East as the perfect opportunity to attempt to do so. As a potentially enormous step in this direction, Mr. Valentine invited the Israeli and Iranian leaders to a Summit. The two countries accepted, and the delegates descended upon Tel Aviv for a meeting.

On the first morning of the meeting, Mr. Valentine greeted Israeli Prime Minister Ehud Olmert and Iranian Mullah Mulani. They got down to business quickly. The three parties spent several hours talking about the tense situation. Mr. Valentine eventually tried to stress the importance of cooperation by stating, "Gentlemen, this may be our only chance to avert a war that could be disastrous for each of your countries. Mr. Olmert, please tell us what Israel wants."

Mr. Olmert replied, "It is very simple, as I have been saying. We will agree to a peace plan if it includes the end of Arab plans to rebuild on the Temple Mount. We insist upon its return to us as a show of good faith."

"No," Mr. Mulani replied before Mr. Olmert could even finish. "We will not abandon plans to rebuild on our Mount."

A pause, and then Mr. Valentine said, "Mr. Mulani. As you know, the Quran says that Jewish people should obey the Torah, and the Torah orders the Jewish people to rebuild the temple on the Temple Mount. Additionally, the Quran does not state that Jerusalem has any significance to your people anyway. The Dome of the Rock was abandoned in 692 AD when Mecca became the destination of the hajj, as it has been ever since."

This gave Mr. Mulani the excuse he had hoped to get to negotiate something away, yet save face and also get something that he really wanted. "I could agree to that," he started, "if we share the Mount. We get the northern half, they get the southern half."

"How does that sound?" Mr. Valentine asked.

"I think that would be acceptable," Mr. Olmert replied.

The two sides worked out the details of that compromise and signed a peace treaty. A major war had been averted. The biggest obstacle and key point in negotiations had been the small, thirty-five acre tract of real estate in downtown Jerusalem; the Temple Mount. It was probably the most famous piece of real estate in the world, and by far the most important. No wonder Steve had been in such awe and wonder when he had walked near that property and gazed up at it not long ago.

The Summit had been a good example of what it says in Zechariah 12:3: "I will make Jerusalem a burdensome stone for all people." This had already been fulfilled throughout history, and especially in the last sixty years. Jerusalem grew up around a village captured by King David from the Jebusites 3,000 years ago, and is now the focal point of never-ending debate among the world's great powers. No other city has been desired and fought over like Jerusalem. In its long history, it has been fought over by armies of the Assyrians, Babylonians, Egyptians, Greeks, Romans, Byzantines, Persians, Arabs, Crusaders, Mongols, Turks, British, Jordanians and more. This is a city that has been besieged about 40 different times and destroyed on 32 different occasions. The rulership of Jerusalem has changed hands 26 times. This happened because Jerusalem sat at the confluence of the major highways that connected Europe, Africa and Asia. Whoever controlled the city could control the Middle East.

More recently, as never before in history, Jerusalem was at the center of world headlines. The nations of the world consider it their responsibility and obligation to meddle in her politics and destiny. Since 1948, Jerusalem has experienced four more wars. Thus, the tiny nation of Israel, with one-one thousandth of the world's population, has occupied one-third of the UN's time. Yes, throughout the UN's history, it had spent one-third of its time debating and voting on issues concerning Israel—quite a burden indeed. Maybe this would not have happened if the UN hadn't always voted against Israel and condemned them for their every action. In fact, 60,000 individual votes had been cast against Israel over the years. That's about 1,000 votes per year against a nation that stands for peace and democracy, but gets hated and blamed for everything. What's done is done though, and that's history. All the eyes of the world were now upon Jerusalem as never before.

In the present, the Summit had accomplished what the world had thought was an impossibility—not only the end of build-up to a major war, but at long last, peace in the Middle East between Israel and its neighbors. The key role of the UN and Mr. Valentine in the historic truce did not go unnoticed. The UN got what it wanted—its status soared overnight when it was able to achieve this peace; the very foundation of the UN charter. It could now return to a position of higher world prominence. As for Mr. Valentine, he had gone from being an unknown to suddenly being well known and in the spotlight the world over. He was hailed as a hero.

Israel got what it wanted—peace which it had sought for decades, and the right to build on part of the Temple Mount, a right it had not had for over 2,000 years.

Iran also got what it wanted—peace. However, Iran had no intention of maintaining the peace. It had only sought peace for a relatively short time before it would be ready to take action. Its intent all along had been to merely seek a peace treaty as long as peace served its purpose and then, in the manner of Yasser Arafat and the legacy he left, break the treaty as it suited them. What's more, Mr. Valentine knew this.

The peace treaty greatly helped Israel continue to recover from the crippling effects of the blast in Jerusalem. The lingering radiation in Jerusalem had long since ended. Now the nation could take another big step forward, forget about war possibilities, and focus on further healing and reconstruction. Rebuilding of the city streets and buildings in the blast area near the Temple Mount had been going on for months. The more complicated issue had been the future of the Temple Mount itself, and that's what the treaty cleared the way for.

Israel had actually been developing plans for construction of a temple on the Temple Mount for years. This had been done in compliance with their direction in the Torah, and in hopes of somehow getting permission to build on the Mount. Building a temple would be the fulfillment of a national dream of the Jewish people and a rallying point and unifying force for the nation's religious and cultural heritage. They had also pursued this in hopes that it could mend the relationship between Muslims and Jews.

The world had been inching for some time toward a single, unified world church, and some people hoped this movement might lead to construction of a temple that represented greater world unity. What better way, it had been thought before the blast, to show and celebrate unity than the Dome of the Rock sitting side-by-side with a Jewish Temple. It had even been proposed that the construction would be a joint venture to show further unity. However, the Arab world had rejected this and all offers before the blast.

The peace treaty removed that roadblock, and now Israel was free to build on their half of the Temple Mount property. The design would not prove to be difficult. They would simply try to duplicate what had been built centuries before when the final temple was constructed by King Herod. Enough historical documents and drawings existed to make the design process fairly simple and quick.

The first step though would be shoring up the Temple Mount foundation which had been weakened by years of Muslim excavations under the Mount, and then weakened more by the bomb blast. Israel was very anxious to do this. The first part of this project would be archaeological digs using the best of new technology, something they had wanted to do for years but were prevented from doing by the Muslims. It is easy to understand why the Muslims had prevented archaeological digs. Digs could undermine Muslim lies proclaiming that Jews have no valid historical roots in the city and its holy sites.

In 2000, Muslims closed off the Temple Mount entirely to any archeological oversight by the Israel Antiquities Authority, yet the Muslims were illegally excavating on the site and purposefully destroying antiquities of immense historical value. They had removed some 13,000 tons of material from the Temple Mount that included archeological remnants from the first and second temples. They dumped the treasures at garbage dumps. Israel has an unblemished record of preserving and protecting the holy sites of all three major religions, but unreported by the mainstream media had been this archaeological vandalism by Arabs that had taken place on and under the Temple Mount for years.

Another reason for the Muslim's actions was their plan to build extensive underground mosques. The intention was to turn the entire Temple Mount compound into an exclusively Islamic site by erasing every sign, remnant, and memory of its Jewish past, including the destruction of archeological findings that are proof of this past. Arafat had indeed planned the elevation of the Temple Mount into an Islamic religious site to rival Mecca and Medina, a further legacy to himself. This was an unprecedented attempt to destroy property and to deny any legitimacy of ancient Jewish heritage in Jerusalem. Their overly aggressive and botched digging to accomplish this had also caused buckling of the southern wall of the Mount, jeopardizing the preservation and future of this enormously historical property for everyone.

It now required top-notch archeological and engineering talent by Israel to safely salvage what they could, but the nation was up to it. It would be a time-consuming project to do it right, but that was their intent.

The temple construction would then start after repairing the foundation. Israel is blessed with some resources, one of them being an abundance of high quality pure white limestone. Israel actually exports it because of the quantity and quality they produce. The temple would be built mainly from this limestone.

During 1982 military action in Lebanon, the Israeli Army discovered and captured huge stores of Russian and Syrian weaponry stored in secret bunkers and tunnels for an invasion of Israel from the north. A large supply of famous Lebanese Cedar wood was also recovered and had been safely stored away for future use in construction of a new temple. The cedar would be used for much of the interior trim, along with gold, silver and bronze.

When completed, the temple would be grand. It would have a large door and be surrounded by many columns. It would face east and have a courtyard in front of it. A wall would enclose the temple and its courtyard. The walls would have gates on each of the four sides.

It had now been several months since the blast. Work was underway under the Temple Mount as crews were beginning the archeological excavations and strengthening the foundation of the Mount. To the delight of most, there were many days when the discovery of significant remains of some sort was announced. Many man-made artifacts were dated as being well over 2,000 years old.

The Van de Kamps decided it was time for them to visit Jerusalem to have a look at things. Steve had not been back since the blast, and Mary and Jeff had not been there yet at all. The family had spent those months trying to let life get back to normal. They were relieved because that seemed to be happening. War would have been very dangerous for any resident of Tel Aviv, a city likely to be targeted.

The family drove to Jerusalem one afternoon. They walked around the Old City. Steve didn't notice many changes, but he did not remember much of how it looked from his single previous visit. Clean-up and reconstruction had mostly been completed, except on the Temple Mount. The gold dome of the Dome of the Rock was no longer there to be seen. The work going on there now was mostly underground on the foundation.

As the family looked up at the hill, Steve read to them from the Bible and said, "Ezekiel was given a vision of the future of the temple which he described in chapter 43: 'I saw the glory of the God of Israel coming from the east. His voice was like the roar of rushing waters, and the land was radiant with his glory. The glory of the Lord entered the temple through the gate facing east and filled the temple. Then the son of man said this is the place of my throne and the place for the soles of my feet. This is where I will live among the Israelites forever. All the surrounding area on top of the mountain will be most holy. Such is the law of the temple.'"

Steve, Mary and Jeff all agreed that it was quite a sight and quite a thought. Despite that clear prophetic vision of the future, though, it was still hard to imagine the power and wrath of what was to come.

———————

Back home in Tel Aviv, life had gotten back to normal for the Van de Kamps. Steve's fifteen minutes of unwanted fame had come and gone. Any thoughts about him possibly being deported had long since vanished. In fact, just the opposite happened—Steve was offered a job by the Israeli government, which was working on its own missile defense system. When Steve's background in missile defense had become widely known, he became a valuable commodity, like a computer hacker who gets caught, slapped on the wrist, and then offered a job because his expertise is recognized. Steve was not only an expert in such matters, but he also knew all about the U.S.'s capability in this field.

The U.S. was the world leader in this technology, but Israel was a close second. Over the years, Israel had bought various missile defense equipment and technology from the U.S. and was now using it, testing it, and trying to improve it. Steve could be invaluable in this process. The close relationship that existed between the U.S. and Israel had made this technology transfer possible. Similar sales and sharing of information had happened for decades between these two allies.

Steve quickly accepted this employment opportunity to get back to work, as he had hoped to do. He made friends with many people at work at a military base in Tel Aviv. He relished the chance to get to know many Israeli residents, especially those at work who knew much about Israeli political and military history. His best friend was a co-worker named Aaron. The two had many long talks together.

Steve found out that Israel, like the U.S., had worked to develop a national missile defense system since the 1980's. Israel's system is called the Arrow Missile Defense System. Israel had an even more pressing need for such a capability than the U.S. since Israel had been the world's largest target of terrorism for decades, which is still true despite 9–11. Israel's technical challenge in this field was smaller than that of the U.S. in that Israel is much smaller. Many of the hurdles the U.S. faced stemmed from its large size, which made the program more technically challenging and expensive. In fact, years ago Israel had become the world's first nation to implement a missile defense system that could protect a whole nation, although the system was far from perfect.

The system had been used in the early 90's during the first Gulf War when Saddam Hussein and Iraq launched many Scud missiles at Israel. Once again, Israel did nothing to provoke a war, a war that Iraq started with Kuwait, yet Iraq was determined to drag Israel in. All Israel did was defend itself by shooting defensive missiles to try to intercept incoming missiles. Out of over 30 Iraqi missiles launched, only a couple got through. The apparent success was later undermined though when it was realized that the Israeli defensive missiles had not been very effective. Instead, it was discovered that the Iraqi Scud missiles were technically poor and had simply broke into pieces upon reentry into the atmosphere.

Israel's system was a start, but it needed improvement. Israel had the engineering capability and funding to continue development. During Steve's first couple of years on the project in Israel, much progress and improvement were made. At one point after a test, Steve's boss, General Oliphant, went to brief the Minister of Defense on where the program stood.

After reviewing the specifics of what had been a successful test, the Minister asked, "It's been three years since we used this system in the real world. Can we rely on it?"

General Oliphant replied, "There are so many variables. What's the speed of the incoming missile? What kind of missile is it? How large is it? Are we successful if we deflect it but don't destroy it? Is an 80% rate acceptable?"

The Minister asked, "Given our perceived threat, is 80% where we are?

"Yes, sir," the general replied. "I'd say we're at 80%. That's putting us up against the full range of possible targets: Scuds, Russian missiles, the whole gamut. Given that, 80% is even more than we thought we'd have at this point."

"Yes," the Minister replied. "I'm satisfied with that for now, but the world is getting more and more dangerous. Your team has done good work, but we face a grave risk. We need to get that number up to 100% as we discussed. Keep at it."

What was the grave risk? The 21st century was still young, but the world had become very dangerous and deadly. There were now 19 wars going on around the world. The number had been going up and was expected to continue to rise. There was something that every one of them had in common: every one involved Muslims attacking a neighbor. The on-going war in Sudan was an example that most people had heard of but knew little about. People assumed it was a civil war, and it was a civil war of the north versus the south, but it began with the Islam-controlled government of the north attacking the Christian south of that nation. For years, Sudan suffered through both war and a carefully manipulated famine. The north had killed at least four million people of the south. Things were now getting worse by spreading to the bordering nations of Uganda and Kenya. The Islamic government wanted the land void of people in order to claim the oil which Sudan is not known for but has much of.

For years, America had done little if anything about the Sudan situation. When asked why many people around the world hate America, one answer is that they have seen the great example of democracy and wondered why, as a world leader, America has accepted to ignore, work with, or even praise corrupt dictators like those in Sudan. History proves that this approach does not work and that appeasement only leads to war. An estimated 170 million people died in the 20th century due to war and famine which were the direct result of the tyrannies of Nazi Germany, Japan, Red China, and the former Soviet Union. Others died in Africa and continue to die every day there because of the tyrants who rule most of its nations. Yet many continued to preach the lies and nonsense of communism and socialism as the answer to the world's problems even though both systems:

- Concentrate power and wealth in government or dictators, rather than allowing the economy to flourish and letting its benefits enrich and enhance the lives of citizens.
- Are less efficient than a capitalist system.
- Are inherently corrupt.

People in every country in the world yearn for the blessings of freedom, liberty and democracy that Americans take for granted. We saw that in 1989 when thousands gathered in Tiananmen Square, the heart of Red China, to protest peacefully for more representative government. The protesters wanted to change their socialist system and to replace it with a Western-style republic. That is why the protesters had created their own Statue of Liberty, but it was crushed beneath the treads of Communist tanks and many were killed by Communist guns.

In a different part of Asia, the challenge in the Middle East was great because none of its 22 Arab countries had ever been a democracy. In the still dangerous Middle East, Bin Laden had not been heard from for some time, but that didn't mean he wasn't planning his next attack. The same thing applied to Iran. Those who knew prophesy were well aware that recent events signaled that much more was to come, and soon.

The Perfect Financial Storm

While the Sudan war and all the other wars raged on, economic problems were ravaging the developed world. The problems started in the United States. This was causing the new American president elected in the 2008 election to mostly ignore foreign wars and other issues to concentrate on handling the serious domestic problems. The numerous economic problems were the result of years of overspending, mismanagement, and putting off the day of reckoning, but that day had finally come.

The origins of the problem went way back. Throughout history, mankind had used gold and silver as money, up until recently that is. The founding fathers of the United States recognized the virtue of gold and silver and implemented a monetary system based upon this by using coins that were actual gold and silver. The paper money was backed by gold and silver in the government's physical possession.

Due to this, the nation had very little monetary problems or inflation with this system until 1913 when the Federal Reserve came into existence. The Federal Reserve is privately owned by member banks; it is not "Federal" and it has no "Reserves." It was charged with managing American mon-

etary policy. However, it has done that as poorly and fraudu-
lently as its name implies—they could not have invented a
more misleading name if they tried. The Federal Reserve's
dire impact would not take long to be seen: very soon came
World War I, then the inflation of the 1920's, and then the
Great Depression of the 1930's that spread worldwide.

As the 20th century went by, the "Fed" and government
made it illegal for Americans to own gold in the 1930's. That
was eventually changed, but then in 1971, they uncoupled
paper money from gold. That meant the nation suddenly
had only "fiat" money, defined as paper money decreed to
be legal tender but not backed by gold or silver or anything
tangible. This was unconstitutional, but they did it anyway.
Why was this done? Simply for power! Gold and silver are
rare because there is only so much of it and it can only be
mined so fast. That's why it was used as money—it has value,
the very definition of money. If the amount of currency in
circulation is restricted so as not to exceed the amount of
gold in the vaults, then the money is worth something.
However, the Fed and government realized there was much
more power in it for them to decouple currency from gold,
so they did so in 1971. This would give them the power to
manipulate the money supply.

The Fed suddenly had power to increase the money supply, and did they ever! The Fed threw an exploding money
supply at every problem that came along. They got the
nation addicted to easy money and easy credit. Back in the
year 2000, debt as a percent of GDP rose to an even higher
level than it was during the Great Depression in the 1930's.
The debt continued to get steadily worse since then. Then
foreign banks got in on the same game too. As if all this
wasn't bad enough, the Fed also:

1. Stopped reporting the unprecedented M-3 money supply growth of well over 10% annually in 2006 to hide their fraud.
2. Invented a highly misleading way of reporting inflation to grossly underreport it to hide their fraud.
3. Started leasing gold in 1998 to skew markets and manipulate gold's price down to hide their fraud.
4. Refused to allow an audit of the gold at Ft. Knox to continue manipulating the market and to hide their fraud.

Are these actions by the Fed really fraudulent? If anyone writes a check backed by nothing, it's fraudulent! The Fed not only did that everyday, but also took these many actions to cover it up.

One of gold's functions is to set off warning flags of coming problems such as inflation, but the Fed stole that tool away from the American public by manipulating the price of gold. The public forgot what the founding fathers knew all too well. The public came to believe that gold was un-American and that it was an unwanted, unneeded, barbarous relic of history. As a result, people didn't see what was coming and suffered when the stock market bubble popped in 2000 and when the housing market bubble popped in 2007. Before popping, these rising asset prices had only created the illusion of wealth anyway because as money becomes more abundant, it's less valuable. The Fed's policy had become one of encouraging debt and causing inflation and hiding it, and they had become masters at it. The public didn't realize that inflation was an intentional, well-designed, hidden tax. The resulting bursting bubbles led to a major worldwide recession.

Steve explained all this to Aaron at work one day. He described this economic history of the U.S. and then said, "That's what started it all and why we're having such problems everywhere. It will probably get worse before it gets better. The world's superpower is in decay and chaos."

Aaron added, "The whole war in Iraq made it worse. It could have been won quickly, but it's like they have no concept of history. Even I know that Vietnam proved that running a police state cannot win a war."

Steve replied, "In 1837, Daniel Webster said 'there is no nation on earth powerful enough to accomplish our overthrow. Our destruction, should it come at all, will be from another quarter; from the inattention of the people to the concerns of their government, from their carelessness and negligence. I fear they may place too much confidence in their public servants and fail to scrutinize their conduct. In this way, they may be made the dupes of designing men, and become the instruments of their own undoing.'"

"It was bound to happen," Aaron said. "It happened to every empire there's ever been…Egypt, Greece, Rome, and Britain."

Steve thought and said, "We became a much stronger nation after Webster said that, but we still found a way to prove him right. Everybody's boundless faith in bigger and bigger government that would always take care of us finally did us in instead. When we moved toward a socialist state, it did us in."

"To that, you added an expensive war. The Soviet Union sealed its own fate in 1980 when it went into Afghanistan and bankrupted itself in the process. Going into Iraq did the same thing to the U.S. Terrorists warned they would kill the dollar, and it seems they did." Aaron was right. "I have a quote for you," Aaron added. "It was your own Thomas Jefferson who said 'The issue today is the same as it has been throughout history, whether man shall be allowed to govern himself or be ruled by a small elite.'"

Steve somberly replied, "In 1835, the French political historian Tocqueville wrote in his *Democracy in America* that 'the American Republic will endure until the day Congress discovers that it can bribe the public with the public's own money.' Sadly, that day has long since arrived."

Aaron added, "Even before that, it was Mayer Rothschild, founder of the Rothschild banking dynasty, who had figured out the key to success when he adroitly said, 'Allow me to issue and control a nation's money, and I care not who makes the laws.' He proved he knew what he was talking about."

The content of these powerful warnings, "being made the dupes of designing men," "the misguided hands of a small elite," and "bribing the public with their own money," displayed the wisdom and forethought of some early Americans and Europeans. On the other hand, the banker Rothschild showed his consuming drive for power, control and greed.

Even before the Fed existed, modern banking forever changed the face of business and commerce when, in one fell swoop, the biblical admonition in Deuteronomy 23:19 and Psalms 15:5 against charging interest on loans was put aside and replaced with a system where interest (usury) formed the very basis of money and exchange. This happened first in England in the 1800's. Their government gave this power to private bankers such as Rothschild to issue money and charge debt. The government gave up this power because they thought that doing so was an acceptable trade-off in their imperialistic goal to wage and win wars. With this ability to finance its military with future debt instead of current savings, England used this modern banking to become the greatest empire the world had ever known by 1850.

However, it soon became clear that bankers got the better end of the bargain as the government and citizens became burdened with increasingly unsustainable levels of debt. By 1870, England's balance of trade turned negative and the cost of maintaining a worldwide military presence drained the British treasury of its gold to pay the debts. By 1900, England's grip on world power was ending and America was rising to replace her.

In a repeat of world history, bankers saw this power shift coming to the U.S. With inside help, they successfully lobbied the Congress and President Woodrow Wilson to institute the Federal Reserve Act of 1913, thereby implementing the exact same system in America that had benefited them so well in England. Before long, President Wilson realized his enormous mistake and conceded that he had unwittingly ruined his country by concentrating the system of credit in the hands of a few men, exactly what Thomas Jefferson had warned against. Since only Congress can issue money, the Act was unconstitutional as it is to this day, but they got away with enacting it anyway.

As in England, it worked for awhile. By 1950, the U.S. was the world's most powerful nation and possessed 75% of the world's gold, the largest amount owned by any nation in history. The face of imperialism had changed somewhat. Instead of being reflected as England's annexing of nations and islands, it now existed as American worldwide domination of banking, currency, and trade. However, just as with England 100 years earlier, circumstances were about to change.

By the 1970's, the U.S. trade balance had turned negative and most of the gold owned in 1950 was gone, sold to temporarily finance America's worldwide military presence and to elevate the U.S. dollar to the status of world currency. By 2000, the U.S., once the world's richest nation, was now the world's largest debtor. In 2006, the Federal Reserve issued a report stating that the gap between future U.S. government receipts and obligations totaled $66 trillion, a sum impossible to reconcile. This meant the U.S. was technically bankrupt, but the few people who noticed did nothing and business went on as usual.

In fact, the government and the Federal Reserve led Americans to believe they were bravely saving the world's economy by being willing to consume with money borrowed from trade partners to buy things not saved for with money that could not be repaid. This is another example of what Adolph Hitler and more recent Muslim leaders did: say anything often enough and people will believe it.

America might have been the most economically illiterate empire in history. The nation had been on the verge of bankruptcy for years, yet most people didn't have the slightest hint of this, or that a crash would have already occurred if not for arm twisting by the U.S. of other nation's central banks to get them to run similarly irresponsible monetary policies worldwide. Thus, the U.S. delayed the inevitable collapse by convincing other countries to increase their money growth rates as fast or faster than the U.S., thereby debasing and devaluing not just the American currency, but all the currencies of the world. A national problem became a worldwide problem.

Steve had seen much of this unfold before his very eyes during his lifetime. First debt became widely acceptable and 30-year home loans became the rule of the land as the Bible's command to cancel debt every seven years was ignored. Then banks invented adjustable rate mortgages, reverse mortgages, zero-down mortgages, home equity loans, subprime loans, and credit cards for everyone to further line the banksters' pockets. Government debt and trade debt created more strains. Debt had long since replaced savings as America's method of business. All the while, the U.S. was losing its industrial base. Taxation rates surged skyward, as though it had been forgotten that this was a main cause of the American Revolution in the first place.

Federal Reserve Chairmen Alan Greenspan and Ben Bernanke did their best jobs at economic double-speak to keep the public in the dark, as did the government regarding all economic topics, such as the depletion of the Ft. Knox gold reserves. American economic policy became an embarrassing mess. For example, China had amassed over $1 trillion in U.S. dollar reserves, and for years they prolonged the life of the U.S. dollar by recycling this trade surplus into U.S. bonds. But now, to add insult to injury and to bite the hand that feeds it, the U.S. slapped China with trade sanctions, which backfired.

For decades, U.S. foreign policy had been heavy-handed economically, financially and militarily, but now the U.S. was failing on all three fronts. The risk of military aggression became bigger and more likely as the economic and financial tools had been weakened by decades of misguided incompetence by the Fed. Now those first two tools no longer worked well so the American weapon of choice became the military option. President Bush was forced to invade Iraq in 2003 to defend the failing dollar, as Steve had discussed with Howard a few years ago.

This most basic principle had been lost on the American public. The inevitable result was the nation and world getting thrown into an economic and military mess. All this resulted because of "modern banking." That's why Thomas

Jefferson had also said, "Banking institutions are more dangerous to our liberties than standing armies."

Steve and Aaron continued their conversation about this. Aaron said, "It sounds like modern banking led to the Federal Reserve, which led to this economic chaos and war. Why isn't the Fed just done away with?"

Steve replied, "Lots of reasons. Whenever an organization is born, its top priority becomes to do all it can to ensure its continued existence. It would take a public outcry, but there's just apathy instead. On top of that, there are two powerful organizations whose function is to continue the control of those few elite who are in power. They are the Council on Foreign Relations and the Trilateral Commission.

"Never heard of them," Aaron said. "What do they do?"

"Almost no one has ever heard of them," Steve said. "Their secrecy is part of what makes them effective." Steve went on to explain the Pandora's Box he had just opened.

Edward House was the chief advisor of President Woodrow Wilson. House was called the most powerful person in the U. S. during the Wilson Administration from 1913 until 1921. In 1912, House stated that he was working for socialism as dreamed of by Karl Marx; his goal was to socialize the U.S. He laid out a plan to control and use both the Democratic and Republican Parties in the creation of a socialist government. To this end, he convinced Wilson to pass the Federal Reserve Act in 1913 which established a private central bank to create and control money, taking this power away from Congress. A graduated income tax as proposed by Karl Marx was also ratified, which started tax rates surging upwards.

In 1921, just before President Wilson left office, House

founded the Council of Foreign Relations (CFR). Its purpose was to continue what House started. The CFR began
to attract men of power and influence. Financing came from
bankers like Rockefeller and Carnegie. At the invitation of
President Roosevelt, members of the CFR gained domination over the State Department in 1940 and maintained it
ever since. The CFR also came to control the CIA.

Presidents Eisenhower, Kennedy, Nixon, Ford, Carter,
Bush, and Clinton were members of the CFR. Some believe
Kennedy became disloyal to the CFR shortly before he was
assassinated. In the CFR's 1978 annual report, it listed 1,878
members, including many Senators and Congressmen and
284 other U.S. Government officials. CFR members run most
of the nation's TV news departments, newspapers and maga-
zines, and dominate the academic world, corporations, huge
tax-exempt foundations, labor unions, the military, and most
segments of American life. For many years, the Chairman of
the Board of this immensely powerful cartel was none other
than banking and oil tycoon David Rockefeller.

A few of these well-known members have stated and
written that the CFR wants to surrender the sovereignty
and national independence of the United States, and to
remove all national boundaries to establish a one-world
socialist government. The one-world government would
then be able to control the areas of finance, business, labor,
education, media and the military. The CFR also wants the
world banking monopoly from whatever power ends up
in the control of global government. To achieve this "globalism," the CFR united the worlds of government, high
finance, big oil, media, trade and commerce.

Barry Goldwater wrote, "It's strange that the Board of
Governors of the Federal Reserve controls the money and
interest rates without the involvement of Congress. The

Federal Reserve, a privately owned organization, has nothing to do with the United States of America!" Those Fed governors are also CFR members, meaning the CFR has more banking control and power than Congress.

Most Americans have never even heard of the Council on Foreign Relations. One reason is because there are hundreds of journalists, correspondents, and media executives who are members of the CFR, but they do not write about the organization. It is an express condition of membership that no one is to disclose what goes on at CFR meetings. This is why the nation's news media, usually aggressive to scoop the competition, remains silent about the CFR, its members and its activities.

A related organization is the Trilateral Commission. Its roots stem from the book *Between Two Ages*, written by Zbigniew Brzezinski in 1970. Just like Edward House decades earlier, Brzezinski praised Marxism and the formation of a one-world government, rejected the Constitution and democratic process, and thought the United States was obsolete. David Rockefeller read this book and founded the Trilateral Commission in 1973 to pursue the same goal—a one-world government. They went a step further than the CFR and made it an international body to better consolidate the world's banking interests and reign in the world's wealth to serve Wall Street banks. Rockefeller appointed Brzezinski to be the Director of the Trilateral Commission.

In 1973, Jimmy Carter became a student of Brzezinski, and a founding member of the Trilateral Commission. Their relationship grew as Carter became president. Carter filled his administration with 300 members of the CFR and the Trilateral Commission. Since then, all presidents have filled their administrations with such members. Some of the current and former members are President Bush's Cabinet,

Dick Cheney, Supreme Court justices, U.S. Senators, Alan Greenspan, Bill Clinton, George Bush Sr., Gerald Ford, Henry Kissinger, George Soros, the President of Mexican American Legal Defense, David Rockefeller, Rupert Murdock and other members of the media.

Barry Goldwater stated, "The Trilateral Commission is international and intends to be the vehicle for worldwide consolidation of commercial and banking interests by seizing control of the government of the United States. It represents a skillful, coordinated effort to consolidate the centers of power—political and monetary." It succeeded in taking over key government decision-making positions.

The results were visible and huge. The Government doesn't always act in the nation's best interest. It doesn't always fight wars to win anymore, such as Vietnam, Lebanon, Somalia, and Iraq. It agrees to international trade agreements and border security policies that are not in the nation's best interest. It does nothing when U.S. jobs and corporate headquarters move overseas. In fact, it practically escorts businesses out the door with excessive taxes and regulations. All this serves their purpose.

The CFR's quarterly journal, *Foreign Affairs*, is the world's most important and influential journal on international relations. It is the mechanism by which the CFR disseminates its game plan to its members. The CFR's positions on core issues are used by politicians to implement policy. Recently proposed was an end to national currencies, and the adoption of just three currencies: one for North America (possibly called the Amero), the Euro, and an Asian currency. This is how the Euro first came into being a decade ago, and is more than a little proof that this process is happening.

Foreign Affairs said the massive U.S. account deficit requires importing $2 billion a day to sustain the dollar's pretense of viability. Reckless U.S. fiscal policy ruined the dollar, and the only way to stave off a global disaster was for countries to join one of these three global currencies. Translation—their plan to fix their mess is to continue a failed "modern banking" system by creating more worthless currencies that will be mismanaged by the same people and the same banking cartel who get rewarded for their elitist networking, secrecy, greed and incompetence with enormous levels of power and income. They ruined England, then they ruined the U.S., now they're making their next move to expand to conquer the world while also ruining it. And by the way, it's another giant step toward their one-world system.

As Steve talked about all this, Aaron sat in near-stunned silence, not quite sure what to believe. Steve realized this and said, "Think about it. This explains so much of what we've been hearing about for years: why Bush often did the opposite of what the public wants, why Senator Reid said we were beaten in Iraq when we weren't, why Clinton did nothing when American interests were attacked abroad for years, why the Clintons tried to socialize healthcare, why Bush did nothing about closing the U.S./Mexico border and wanted to turn over U.S. seaport security to Arab-run Dubai Ports, why they desperately wanted to give citizenship to illegal aliens, why Clinton shrank the U.S. military and paid a terrorist network, why no one did anything about the serious financial trouble we were hurtling toward, why the U.S. signed agreements like NAFTA to suck jobs away, why no one ever discusses the Fed's incompetence or sovereignty, and why liberals do all they can to weaken us in every way like loathing the military and making us dependent on foreign oil."

Steve paused a moment and then continued, "The banking tycoons don't care about the political ramifications because they still make a fortune, and just like Rothschild said, it's all because bankers control the money supply. It also takes us right down the same path the bible says the antichrist will take the world—toward one world government and one world currency. They're helping that along right before our very eyes. It's amazing; it's scary; and they keep getting away with it!"

"Yeah, I'll say," Aaron eventually uttered. "You Americans should wake up and take your country back, especially since you're ruining foreign economies and taking down far more than just yourselves."

Steve conceded and said, "As the world watches and does nothing, the bankers are slowly building and controlling a new world order to safeguard their financial empire while they ruin every nation. To top it off, they call it 'public service.' It's really nothing but lies."

When the Fed reacted to the stock market crash of 2000–2001 and 9–11's economic downturn with a money supply explosion and 1% interest rates, the world became awash in unbacked dollars. This caused asset and finance bubbles worldwide. It was easy to see major problems coming as a result, although very few did so.

Eventually, the housing market bubble burst in 2007, as reflected by rising levels of home foreclosures, slowing sales, falling prices and much more. This started the economic ball rolling down a steep hill over the next few years, compounded by mounting military costs and other spending, rising oil prices, bankruptcies, a credit crunch, geopolitical problems, and eventually failing hedge funds and

$400 trillion of collapsing derivatives. The public no longer believed false inflation statistics. Many foreign countries no longer accepted depreciating American dollars and depreciating Treasury bonds in exchange for their real goods, so the dollar fell more as countries realized the futility of a debt-based fiat currency.

The stock market had been supported for years by the government's "plunge protection team," which also kept a lid on the price of gold. No matter how well conceived though, manipulations always end, and end badly. Sure enough, gold broke from its shackles and climbed to all-time highs over $1,000. Then the International Monetary Fund (IMF) caused the first public audit in over 50 years of the gold in Ft. Knox, Kentucky. It was finally revealed that the leased gold was gone and not recoverable. The cover-up was over and gold exploded further in price.

The political embarrassment and fall-out from that manipulation and cover-up caused endless time and money to be wasted in court and Congressional hearings to investigate. This was all because an economic fact of history had been ignored: every fiat money system eventually fails because money created out of thin air is toilet paper, not a storehouse of value. Genesis 2:12 says "The gold of the land is good." At the very beginning, before the Bible even mentions Adam and Eve, it said that "gold is good." It never says that about dollars. It never says that about paper money. What it said about gold never changed, but the government thought it knew better. Proverbs 22:7 says, "The borrower is servant to the lender," but people didn't mind throwing themselves into this disastrous subservient predicament where it was the banks that actually owned their houses and cars.

The IMF's audit news from Ft. Knox told the world that the value of American dollars it was holding was much less than thought. America's biggest creditors, China and Japan, sold their American bonds. America's trade and federal budget deficits had teetered on the edge of disaster for years and were now pushed over the edge, further adding to the problems.

This led to a worldwide panic. The dollar plunged. Stocks in the U.S. and on worldwide markets plunged. The nation and then the world were thrown into a depression. Baby boomers who thought they couldn't afford to retire yet got laid off, as did many others of all ages. Offers of cheap loans did not attract confidence-stricken people who saw prices on some things like houses falling and waited for lower prices. It was a vicious cycle—no buying led to layoffs leading to no product demand leading to lower prices leading to lower profits leading to more layoffs and so on. Japan had been through this in the 90's, and now the whole world was feeling the same pain.

Gold was the only investment class that went up since it is the only real storehouse of value. Reaching $1,000 was nothing since gold had to reach $2,500 to equal its inflation adjusted high of $850 in 1980, so it continued upward. Anybody with a sense of reality or a little historical perspective knew this, saw it coming, and had prepared to benefit accordingly.

America thought it was immune from a depression. The Fed and media had spread this fabricated story of immunity since it said its new tools and knowledge would prevent a repeat of the 1930's depression, but this story was another fraud by the Fed scam to keep itself in power. They actually did have the economic tools and lessons of history available, but their greed, secrecy and incompetence got in the way again. Congress should have seen this coming, but loved spending money they didn't have and loved getting votes instead, so they did nothing to prevent this. Congress was also caught up in their normal feuds and scandals instead of doing their jobs.

In the 1980's, the U.S. just had to patiently wait while the Soviet Union imploded, which it did. Now for the last several years, terrorists had warned that they would destroy the dollar. How ironic it was that they just needed to wait patiently while the U.S. did that for them. The actions of the Federal Reserve, the Council on Foreign Relations and the Trilateral Commission led to the war and a weaker U.S. and were also causing the world's economic woes.

With the actions of those three organizations, it was as though the terrorists had infiltrated the upper levels of control of the U.S. because the resulting economic chaos was exactly what they wanted. Terrorists getting what they wanted was nothing new of course; they had been getting massive Western payments for their oil for decades. Instead of drilling the huge oil deposits in Alaska and just off its own shores, America had depended on the Middle East and Venezuela for oil; another huge example of inexplicable government action, and the move toward globalism that contributed to all this.

The countries that withstood the depression the best were those with natural resources, an economy built on manufacturing and wise investment, and a currency that was at least partially backed by gold. Russia was one such country, mostly due to their resources. They thought the time was now at hand to take full advantage of their resources, specifically their natural gas. Back in 2006, Russia had literally cut off the flow of natural gas to Ukraine with the flip of a switch at Gazprom headquarters in Moscow. This was done when Ukraine ousted their pro-Russian president in a democratic election. Not by coincidence, this happened in the middle of winter in a country known for severe winters. Ukraine had to agree to pay Russia ten times the previous price to restart the flow of gas.

Now Russia decided to do the same thing to all their European customers. They began requiring exorbitant prices from European countries and threatened them with no gas if they did not comply. The Russian near-monopoly in gas had never been broken in recent years. The European nations imported 60% of their natural gas making them as a whole the world's largest importer of the fuel. Their alternative sources could not nearly make up the difference. Iran was one of those other sources, but Iran had decided in advance to help their ally, Russia, by not increasing the amount it exports.

A source of heat in the winter is like food—even if you're down to your last few dollars, that's what the dollars get spent on while people find a way to go without everything else. Europe had been hit by the same worldwide economic woes affecting every other country. The last thing it needed was this additional shortage and further cause of inflation.

The European Union (EU) held an emergency meeting at its headquarters in Brussels. Ten nations stepped forward to take a leadership role in this matter. They jointly agreed that severe gas price inflation was actually the next to last thing it needed; a heating gas shortage was the last thing and would be even worse. A shortage of this critical heating source in winter would probably cause deaths among the elderly and rioting by everybody else.

The European nations agreed to the enormous hikes in fees, but knew they had been blackmailed, were not happy, and decided to do something about it. They held a series of talks among themselves and discussed options like trade sanctions with Russia, and even the possibility of war.

Before they ever came to a joint agreement on a plan to proceed with, their worst fears materialized. The huge price increase had to be passed along to the public, and many people simply couldn't afford to pay it. Some of the elderly died, some moved away, some moved in with relatives, and others just moved out of their cold homes and sought public shelters. There was widespread outcry over lack of government help.

The quickly worsening situation led to riots, similar to what Paris experienced for several brutal, destructive weeks in 2005. Those riots had been over a small segment of the Muslim population being unhappy about access to jobs. These new riots were much larger and were occurring with regularity in most cities on the European continent.

The politicians realized their indecision had to change. Again, the same 10 member nations stepped forward to provide the needed leadership: Spain, Portugal, Italy, Germany, the United Kingdom, Belgium, Finland, Sweden, Poland and Greece. Thanks to the near panic situation, they agreed to join forces militarily, and to demand Russian cooperation or they would take military action.

It took this to make Europe realize the power they had when its nations cooperate. For years, the combined nations of the EU had been the world's largest economic power, but they never really capitalized on the power this could have given them. In time, this newfound cooperation could lead to a stronger EU, but for now, the big question was how Russia would respond to this.

Before Europe got an answer though, disaster struck. Back at their home in Tel Aviv, Mary and Steve turned on the TV one morning to see a special news report. A huge earthquake had occurred, centered in the Gulf of Finland. It registered 9.5 on the Richter scale, making it the second largest quake in recorded history, now ahead of the previously second largest quake on Dec 26, 2004 in the Indian Ocean which had registered 9.3. The Gulf of Finland is small, which is the reason most people have not heard of it. Unfortunately, quite close by are the major cities of Helsinki, Finland and St. Petersburg, Russia (formerly Leningrad). The two cities are less than 200 miles part. Both cities suffered the deaths of thousands of people and widespread damage.

St. Petersburg is the larger of the two cities and experienced more damage. Maybe fittingly, St. Petersburg suffered severe damage to its infrastructure, especially its gas system, and now its citizens were without the necessities of life like a source of heat. Help was slow in coming to both cities and the many other smaller cities nearby due to the widespread nature of the damage which made search and rescue and clean-up harder, especially with the lack of utilities and cold weather in this far north location.

The world heard news about the aftermath of the huge earthquake for days to come as rescue and clean-up efforts continued. Also in the news was a worsening situation in Africa where a drought had been on-going for a couple of years. News of the resulting famine was now spreading, as were deaths from starvation and disease.

The earthquake momentarily put the Russian-European hostilities on hold, but the world was suffering from brutal wars elsewhere as well as economic and natural disasters, and the worst was yet to come.

ATTACK

The world was awash in turmoil and problems, both man-made and natural. Ironically though, the Middle East had been relatively quiet for three years since the peace plan was signed between Israel and Iran. Iran had agreed to this plan though only as a way to buy time. The strike by Israel against Iran's nuclear development facilities three years ago had done its job well and set Iran's nuclear program back considerably, and Iran needed time to recover. That recovery was more than underway.

Meanwhile, Osama bin Laden and his al-Qaeda network were as strong as ever. Al-Qaeda and Iran had developed strong bonds with each other. Both had been planning and preparing their next strike. Now that world governments had shifted priorities and were focusing more on economic problems than on security, the enemies of the civilized world were ready to make their next move. They had planned an immense one-two punch to the United States. Blow number one was to wreak financial havoc, which happened. Blow number two was even bigger, and its time had now come.

Since the time in 2007 when Randy Bomar filmed Steve in California during the missile test, Bomar had returned to the Middle East to remain in hiding and await his next assignment. He had recently returned to the U.S. via Mexico for that next task whose time had come.

In Southern California one night, Bomar drove his vehicle up the Pacific Coast Highway. He stopped at a seaside parking lot in the beach town on El Segundo, a Los Angeles suburb. He pulled something large out of the back of his vehicle. It was not his camera equipment this time; it was a rocket-propelled grenade launcher (RPG), armed with an explosive warhead. There was only the highway to his north and south, nothing but ocean to the west and just a small hill to the east. Without a person, building or even a house in sight, what was he doing?

The answer came screaming overhead just a minute later. Bomar had set-up shop just off the western edge of the runways of Los Angeles International Airport. As usual, the wind was blowing easterly off the ocean, so the planes were taking off westbound, reaching the ocean's edge within seconds after take-off. Anyone who knows planes can tell what type of plane is coming by the sound of the engines. This plane and the next one were not what Bomar was waiting for. The third plane was. It was a larger plane—a 767 widebody that carried more people, the same type of plane that al-Qaeda commandeered two of and destroyed on 9–11.

Bomar's relatively simple weapon did not have high-tech heat-seeking or infrared capability. It was more like a bazooka; aim and fire and hope you have aimed well. In the hands of a skilled user though, RPG's have an effective range of about 1,000 feet, good enough for this situation. Just seconds after take-off, any large aircraft is a big, slow-moving target and still low to the ground. Take-offs are sometimes described as people being packed in a metal tube with few exits and surrounded by huge quantities of explosive fuel while hurtling along at ever higher speed to the point of no return; always a potential disaster.

Bomar aimed his launcher skyward. He was ready and calmly pulled the trigger. The grenade rocketed upward and hit the massive fuselage. Planes are engineered to withstand certain high stresses, but the rocket penetrated the aircraft's skin. The pilot, crew and passengers were helpless. The disastrous result was inevitable. The aircraft quickly became a fireball and before long exploded into a million pieces. The sky rained down an endless stream of debris from the plane, all of it falling into the Pacific Ocean which would make recovery all the more difficult. Two hundred and fifteen people had their lives come to a very quick and unexpected end that night.

The explosion was seen and heard by many people on the patios and porches of their expensive homes from Malibu to the Palos Verde Peninsula and all the beach towns in-between. The airborne disaster was eerily reminiscent of TWA Flight 800, a 747 that exploded in similar fashion in 1996 just after take-off from New York City when it was flying low over ocean waters near Long Island on the other side of the country.

Al-Qaeda had prepared a video about their newest attack that it now released through Al Jazeera. In it, terrorists proudly proclaimed their responsibility for this newest round of terrorism. The video's real purpose though was now revealed. The terrorists warned that no one could stop them from repeating elsewhere what they had just done in Los Angeles, and that all Muslims should get out of the Great Satan and the Little Satan before it was too late!

That warning was actually a distraction from what was to come next. The message was designed to get security forces focused on air travel again, and away from other security concerns. It worked quite well.

Iran had acquired multiple small nuclear bombs from Russia, but had decided not to use any more of them yet since the one that was used in Jerusalem. What Iran now sought was the development or acquisition of a larger nuclear bomb on the order of at least 30 kilotons. Their suitcase bombs acquired from Russia, in comparison, were just 0.1 kilotons. They tried to buy larger bombs from Russia but had been refused. Russia saw what Iran had done with a smaller bomb in Jerusalem and did not want to be implicated in anything further. Russia had many large nuclear bombs for decades throughout the Cold War. They never used them though, mostly due to the concept of mutually assured destruction—using one against the United States would have meant a U.S. nuclear retaliation and the widespread destruction of each country. It was a deterrence that had worked well for each country.

The U.S. had used two nukes in Japan to end World War II, but seemed justified in doing so during a state of war against Japan who had attacked an unprovoked U.S. at Pearl Harbor. America also hoped that use of the two bombs would end the war and save lives in the long run. That turned out to be the case. The world had never seen anything though like the situation in Jerusalem where a nuclear bomb had been used offensively by Iran against Israel with no provocation.

Now, more nuclear bombs were in the hands of religious fanatics who were seized with an end-of-the-world eschatological belief. They felt it was their divine duty to hasten this apocalypse. As their own president had announced to the world a few years earlier, it was also their duty and ambition to annihilate Israel, and he didn't care if it caused the death of half of his countrymen to achieve that goal. The concept of mutually assured destruction (MAD) no longer applied in this case. Russia was aware of this so they would not sell Iran any more bombs, but Russia hadn't told the world about Iran's intentions.

This did not deter Iran; it merely caused them to change their game plan. Furthermore, they were greatly aided by Russian nuclear scientists from the Cold War days who had become unemployed. Iran had paid them handsomely for many years now to assist Iran in the development of both a nuclear capability and the missile technology to deliver a bomb. With this assistance, Iran had resumed their nuclear development program.

After three years of preparation, they had completed their first large bomb. So intent were they on proceeding with a strike against Israel as soon as possible that they sought a way to strike a lethal blow immediately without waiting any longer for additional bombs to be completed and available. Israel is not a large country, but it was large enough that a single nuclear bomb, even this very large, 30-kiloton bomb, could only destroy about half the country.

Iranian military strategists proposed a plan to overcome this "problem." They proposed launching the single nuke toward Israel and intentionally detonating it while it was still airborne. They explained how this would send an electromagnetic pulse (EMP) out from the blast site. This pulse would contain tremendous electrical energy that would destroy the electrons in everything it hit.

When asked what it would hit, they responded that it would hit everything within the field-of-view of the blast. This applied whether the blast occurred in the atmosphere or even in space, no matter how high up. The higher up, the larger it's field-of-view and the wider the destruction.

When asked to describe the destruction, they explained

that the impact would be huge. The pulse doesn't kill or injure people, but the result is nevertheless devastating. Everything electrical seen and hit by the pulse would get zapped and irreversibly damaged and rendered useless. Think of it. No electrical infrastructure. No lights. No computers. Cars and planes wouldn't work due to batteries not working along with every other electrical component being dead. No media. No communications. No military command and control, along with no tanks. It's the perfect weapon. The whole country would be rendered helpless and readily vulnerable to any army that wants to move in and take over. A bomb exploded about 30 miles up in space over Israel would provide the right "footprint" to effect the whole country.

Iran's leadership liked this idea so they consulted with some of their top scientists and engineers to verify what they had heard. They were told that the scientific principles behind generating a high-altitude EMP have been known about since the 1940's and are relatively simple. If a nuclear weapon is detonated between 25 miles and 300 miles above the earth's surface, the radiation from the explosion interacts with air molecules to produce high-energy electrons that speed across the earth's magnetic field as an instantaneous, invisible electromagnetic pulse that destroy everything electrical in their path.

An EMP can have devastating consequences for developed countries because any metallic conductor in the affected area becomes a "receiver" for the powerful energy burst released by the blast. Such receivers include anything with electronic wiring—from airplanes and automobiles to computers, railroad tracks, and communication lines. If systems connected to these receivers are not protected with hardening, they will be damaged or disrupted by the intense energy pulse. An EMP attack damages or destroys all unprotected electronic equipment within the blast's line of sight or footprint on the earth's surface. The size of the footprint is determined by the altitude of the explosion. The higher the altitude, the larger the land area affected.

Any developed nation like Israel depends hugely on electrical products for everyday life, not to mention its military capabilities. Removing electrical capabilities and machines would set a nation back by over a hundred years and render anything more complicated than riding a bicycle impossible. It would make Israel a sitting duck for Iran's army to roll in and wipe it out.

Iran had joined the nuclear "club" as it had sought to do for years. It was not interested in using its new-found capability for power generation purposes or military defensive purposes. It was interested in doing what it had told the world it was going to do—annihilate Israel, and then go after the West too. Furthermore, Iran had vastly improved its Scud ballistic missiles that would work for delivery of a payload into the lower reaches of space.

It was decided to launch the missile from a ship in the Arabian Sea which borders the southern part of Iran. Launching from there instead of from land, it was reasoned, might make it more difficult to identify who had launched the missile. The day for launch was selected, and it was also decided to launch the missile just after darkness; what better way to throw the target into maximum chaos than to have the lights go out at night, among many other major problems that would be experienced.

They had a point. Israel is probably better prepared than any other country for a nuclear explosion or chemical attack. They have many fallout shelters and gas masks and hold many drills for such an attack. However, preparing for the potential of no power is something they had never really considered or prepared for. Simply being in near total darkness would add to the many, many problems Israel would face, if the attack worked.

The mullahs prayed often for the success of the attack they had planned, all the while thinking it was ordained as their destiny and duty to perform such an attack. One nation had decided to launch their first and only nuclear missile, sent on a mission that represented most Middle Eastern countries, a religion, a part of the world, and a way of life; a way of life that they wanted to impose on the world. The stakes could not have been much higher.

An Iranian ship that carried the nuclear-tipped missile cut through the waters of the Arabian Sea not far off Iran's southern coastline. On a hot day in June, at 9:00 PM local time, the ship's commander entered the code that armed the nuke. He then pressed the red launch button. With a loud roar and a cloud of smoke, the large, supersonic missile rocketed skyward flawlessly into the summer night. It was now en route on its mission that would take it on a path west by northwest toward coordinates over the center of Israel where it would detonate 30 miles up in space, an altitude of about 158,000 feet.

Another feature of this attack that the planners loved was the fact that there was no risk of the rocket even having to come back down through the atmosphere, the problem that had done in many Iraqi launches in the 90's. The missile had to go about the equivalent of the distance from New York City to Denver, which it would cover in about 12 minutes.

At this moment at an Israeli military base in Tel Aviv, several people were on duty working in the command and control room of Israel's missile defense system. Steve and Aaron were two of the men on duty. It's a job that is often far more monotonous than exciting, but tonight would soon be quite unique and anything but monotonous. For now, the two men were talking about the merits of soccer versus American football. Steve had now been in Israel for a few years and missed some things from back home like American sports. He was engaged in conversation with Aaron and was promoting the excitement of football as compared to the "excitement" of a scoreless tie in soccer.

Suddenly, a siren sounded in the control room. Every man there instantly knew what it meant: that radar sites on the ground and/or satellite tracking systems saw a missile in flight. Every man there also knew what they were supposed to do. Steve and Aaron looked at their computer screens and scopes in front of them. In just a matter of seconds, they were able to tell what had caused the alarm. They could see the flight path of a missile, headed from east to west, straight toward their country. They didn't know who had launched it, but that didn't matter for now, although they did know it had not been launched by any ally of theirs since they had not been informed of any test or exercise activity going on that day.

With the speed of modern missiles, there was not much time to waste. Steve loudly informed the officer in charge of the situation by stating, "Colonel Cormier, we have an inbound missile."

The colonel quickly walked over to confirm for himself what Steve had seen.

There was much activity for a few seconds but no one spoke until Steve said "Sir, shall we fire?"

The colonel did not respond right away. With great concentration and not a hint of panic in his eyes, he paused for just a moment and continued to gaze intently on the screens in front of him. The screens told him all he needed:

The missile's current location: The Gulf of Oman
Altitude: 110,000 feet and slowly climbing
Heading: three-zero-zero degrees

Much training had gone on among these personnel for years for a moment like this. There was no need to call anyone up the chain of command to get permission to take action; no time either.

After fifteen seconds, the colonel gave Steve his response, "Fire. Repeat…fire."

Steve looked down at his controls and initiated the launch sequence. The final switch he threw caused a lone missile to ignite its engines and launch itself. From its silo in the ground about 15 miles outside of the city, the single missile roared to life and flew into the night sky, just like the enemy's missile had done hundreds of miles away just two or three minutes ago.

The silo had a video camera fixed on it that was able to be monitored back at the control room. Colonel Cormier, Aaron, Steve and the others could see that it looked like a perfect launch. Just like that, their work was done. The missile's tracking and guidance system would take over from there, with the continuing automatic assistance of the same ground radars and satellite tracking that had identified the enemy missile in the first place.

All this equipment working together was the result of years of complicated engineering development and testing which was now seamlessly working with perfect results, so far. That's in fact what would be needed—perfect results—on a mission where so much could go wrong and so much was at stake.

The missile was beyond the range of the TV camera within seconds so the crew at the control center could not monitor the missile's path visually, but they could track its progress by telemetry on computer monitors. All eyes were upon the monitors that were clearly showing the progress of the two missiles as they approached each other; one heading east and one heading west at high speed.

Colonel Cormier used this moment to place a call to General Oliphant, who was at home. "General," he began, "We have an emergency situation. We have an inbound enemy missile. We launched an interceptor back at it."

"What's the status now?" the general asked.

"We're tracking things real-time right now sir," the colonel replied. "The activity is east of us. We're getting perfect telemetry. We should have intercept in about two minutes."

"Can you tell what kind of missile it is?" General Oliphant asked.

"No. We just know that its heading has had it coming straight toward us since it was launched."

"I'll stay on the line. Give me an update in a minute," the general said as he set that phone down to call his superior.

For the next minute there was plenty of talking going on in the control room, although some of it was people talking out loud to themselves as they waited and wondered what would happen. The two missiles were clearly visible on the radar scopes as they raced toward each other.

And then…they met. Direct hit! The Arrow interceptor missile's guidance system worked perfectly and the missile hit its target. Both missiles disappeared from the scopes. The telemetry from the Arrow stopped, and the telemetry from the GPS satellite verified that the missiles no longer existed. The control room erupted with shouts of joy and relief.

The years and years of work had successfully come together to make an enormous difference in the defense of the homeland. The successful use of an Arrow missile in a real-world crisis had just occurred. The probability of this had been estimated at about 80%, but while the Arrow was tracking the Iranian Scud, the engineers couldn't help but think about the dozens of things that could go wrong. The system had been designed to fix and prevent these problems that had been discovered in testing, but suddenly the 80% estimate of something happening successfully that had never happened before under these conditions seemed optimistically high.

Nevertheless, their missile defense system had just shot down an enemy's advanced-technology missile, one that was loaded for the first time with a very large nuclear payload.

Was a disaster averted? Did the enemy have a back-up plan? The enemy was far more than just Iran. It was also all those nations, sects and people who sought to destroy the West, Israel, freedom and democracy. This included bin Laden and his network. Bin Laden was well aware of what Iran had attempted. He had helped with their planning, and what's more, he had an even more lethal plan well underway that same night.

The bombing of the aircraft in Los Angeles a month earlier and subsequent video had indeed been a warning for Muslims to flee America and Israel before the big attack that had started that night. It was not over yet. Dual attacks had been planned to cause more damage and more psychological impact, and in case one attack should fail, the other might succeed. After years of planning, another blow to defeat the West was now in progress.

A cargo ship had been sailing for the last three days from Venezuela, bound for New York City. The ship had just sailed under the Verrazano Narrows Bridge and past the Statue of Liberty. It was now getting pushed by tugboats into its dock amidst the sprawling shipyards of Manhattan's lower west side that run adjacent to the West Side Expressway between the Lincoln and Holland Tunnels. Before long the ship was in place, had shut down its engines and was being tied to the dock.

A little while later, the Harbor Master met with the ship's captain and reviewed the ship's documentation. Something suspicious caught the Master's attention and he proceeded to question the captain about his crew. The captain was told that his cargo could not be off-loaded until the morning, after the ship was inspected that night. The captain asked why and put up a small fight, but then relented. An hour later, the captain had left and found a private spot from which to place a call on his cell phone.

A short time later, the detonation device on a 10-kiloton nuclear bomb that had been well-hidden in the cargo hold of that large ship was activated. Seconds later, the bomb detonated.

The ball of fire from the bomb rapidly expanded to a radius of several hundred feet just one second after the blast. The bomb generated a huge wave of enormously high pressure air which moved outward from the center of the explosion. This shock wave moved with the speed of sound and caused major damage, soon reaching a radius of almost ten miles. The striking feature in the sky was the rise of the ball of fire at the rate of 100 feet per second. After the first minute, the fireball expanded to a radius of many hundreds of yards and rose to a height of about one mile. The ball then lost its brilliance and appeared as a great cloud of smoke lit from within, the result of the pulverized material of the bomb and everything around it. The cloud continued to rise and mushroomed out at an altitude of 25,000 feet. The cloud eventually reached a height of 50,000 feet in the next thirty minutes.

Back down on the ground, the face of America's largest city had changed forever. The explosion occurred within the hull of the ship which helped decrease the damage a little, but you'd never know it. The pressure wave collapsed all buildings within two thousand feet of ground zero. Beyond that, many other buildings also came down, although newer, reinforced buildings designed to withstand earthquakes fared better. Even those had windows blown out though and many suffered fire damage. Near the blast site, fires started instantaneously from the heat. Secondary fires started due to collapsed buildings, damaged electrical and gas lines, overturned stoves, and the like.

Almost everything was destroyed within one mile of the explosion. Nearly everything was damaged within three miles of the blast; from the southern tip of Manhattan to Central Park. This included such landmarks and business centers as Wall Street, the Empire State Building, New York University, Greenwich Village, Little Italy, Chinatown, Madison Square Garden, the NY Public Library, Radio City Music Hall and Carnegie Hall, the Lincoln Center for the Performing Arts, the Museum of Art, Rockefeller Center, St Patrick's Cathedral, and the United Nations. Beyond this distance, damage was lighter but extended for several more miles. Glass was broken up to 10 miles away. The same thing was true across the Hudson River in Jersey City and Newark, New Jersey.

Much of the area is residential so the death toll was

extraordinary. The massive casualties were due to so many factors: the pressure wave, flash burns caused by the heat and light at the moment of the explosion, burns resulting from the secondary fires, the collapsed buildings, flying debris, and finally, by radiation from the nuclear explosion. Almost one-tenth of the city's huge population was killed that day, and an additional one-fifth suffered injuries. In the next years to come, scores more would die from the radiation exposure.

For now though, search and rescue would be not just be hard but impossible. Many policemen and firemen were victims. Nearby hospitals were destroyed or damaged. The infrastructure was destroyed. Radiation fears would keep people away. Streets were inaccessible anyway.

Bin Laden's plan had been simple yet solid for this operation dubbed "American Hiroshima." The only hard part had been getting a nuke. He had accomplished that years ago though, and then devoted years to planning and preparations since then. Bin Laden had hated New York City as a symbol of America for years. His success there on 9–11 had caused him to come back for more. The nature of New York as a target made it irresistible—all those people and all those buildings crammed together right on the edge of the water with few if any barriers to stop a well-executed attack. Bin Laden had also been fascinated by the aftermath of 9–11 when he watched American reports about how the World Trade Center's foundation went down 80 feet below the street level. It was reported that damage to the foundation could allow water to enter from the nearby Hudson River and cause more buildings to collapse. This gave bin

Laden the idea for this attack from the water's edge years ago. The time had come, and it had worked.

A huge nuclear explosion had just rocked a vital and heavily populated city. Meanwhile, what had happened in the sky over the Middle East in a different part of the world? What would the effects be? Who would take charge? Would it be every country for itself? Would the civilized world survive?

Two Regions Shut Down

For the enemy, the attacks could not have gone much better than it did in New York City, or much worse than it did in the Middle East where the bomb intended for Israel exploded over Kuwait instead. Bin Laden had picked his favorite target, the U.S., and succeeded. Iran had picked its favorite target, Israel, and failed.

Israel has had much experience with attacks before. In the first Gulf War in the early 1990's, Saddam Hussein and Iraq shot missiles into Israel. Much less known at the time was that Hussein and Iraq also planned to send fighter and bomber aircraft to hit Israel with chemical bombs. This was thwarted though by the speed with which U.S. forces decimated Iraq's Air Force. Had Iraq been able to proceed with its bombing plan, Israel was prepared to send its aircraft to attempt to intercept and destroy the enemy planes over Jordan and Syria without ever letting the danger of the chemical bombs get over Israeli airspace. Just like the U.S. had not wanted the war on terrorism to be brought to the U.S. and fought on its own soil, Israel likewise did not want chemical bombs in, over or near its country.

As a result of the 90's experience, Israel also knew long

ago that Hussein had weapons of mass destruction; the same weapons that he used on Iran in the 80's; the same weapons that he used on his own people throughout his dictatorship to kill at least 70,000; the same weapons that he was prepared to use against Israel in 1991. Had planes laden with chemical bombs been destroyed over Jordan or Syria in 1991, who knows what might have happened in terms of the fall-out from the chemical bombs?

For this and many more reasons, Israel had spent much time, effort and money since then redesigning and improving its missile defense system based upon what they had learned about the grave threats posed, and the enemy's ability and desire to carry out their threats. Instead of ignoring a known threat, they mitigated the threat. The work had just paid off big time for Israel.

The United States, however, had known for years that only 5–10% of cargo ship contents got inspected; the same thing applied to aircraft cargo. Not one to fix things until it's too late whether it was a financial or military threat, the U.S. did nothing to mitigate its known threat and had just paid the ultimate price.

Had Iran's nuclear bomb successfully detonated over Israel, what would have happened? The world was about to find out what can happen when a nuclear-armed missile gets shot down while airborne. The nuclear bomb did detonate when Iran's Scud missile got hit by the Arrow. Thirty miles above the earth up in space it detonated. It detonated with all the fury that a large nuclear device can unleash. This happened at the altitude it had been programmed to happen at, just a few minutes sooner than the enemy planned. The explosion happened over Kuwait, a small, oil-rich country that is surrounded by Iraq, Iran, Saudi Arabia and the Persian Gulf.

As expected, the large nuclear blast caused a powerful EMP. At the altitude of 158,000 feet, the blast's footprint extended for about 130 miles in all directions on the earth below. It happened in an instant. No one dropped dead since the blast had no effect on people, but it was as though the atmosphere had rained down instant chaos on everything electrical in this region. Everything within a circle on earth of approximately 260 miles in diameter was hit by a powerful electromagnetic shock wave. Instantly, everything electrical stopped working. Power generation came to an end and electrical grids shut down. All electrical devices were instantly zapped and would not work. Even if a power generation station was nuclear-hardened and could still produce and distribute electricity, electrical devices would no longer work unless they too were hardened, and very little was.

Any part of the world inside this circle that had come to rely on electricity for modern-day life was instantly thrown back over 100 years by this phenomenon. This happened in parts of Iraq, Iran and Saudi Arabia and all of Kuwait. In an instant, all electrical power suddenly disappeared. Lights went out and houses and buildings went dark. Refrigerators, computers, televisions, air conditioners, traffic lights and everything else suddenly went dead and dark. Cars and trains stopped running. Planes flying in the region lost power and fell from the sky.

Millions of people were suddenly thrown into a state of chaos. They did not even know what had happened. TV and radio stations were knocked off the air. Even if stations had been able to transmit emergency broadcasts, they had yet to figure out what had happened or what to do, plus TVs and radios were not working anyway.

The people in the large region affected by the EMP from the nuclear blast could see the results of what had happened, but they did not know what had happened or why. It was back in Israel where people first realized what had happened. In the Arrow's control room, Aaron had moved to a different scope. He then approached his superior and said, "Colonel Cormier, come look at this."

"What is it?" the colonel asked as they walked toward a monitor.

"It's nothing, just nothing," Aaron replied. "I mean, east of here where the blast occurred, it's just darkness. Look here."

The colonel looked at the monitor that shows airborne aircraft in a large region and saw nothing, a situation that never occurs. "What does this mean?" he asked.

Aaron grimly answered, "They've lost power, sir. Every plane in that region is down. It wouldn't be from the blast itself, but from an EMP. At that altitude, the footprint would cover at least 200 miles. That means they've lost all electrical power in an area at least that large. But that's 700 miles from here so our nation is not affected. Jordan and Syria are also safe, but Kuwait and her neighbors got hit."

Colonel Cormier said out loud as though thinking, "A real world EMP. Not a theoretical study, but the real thing. The world will find out that an EMP causes irreversible damage. The devices don't come back on-line in a minute or two like we see in the movies. This will wreak havoc, but we had no choice. They forced the issue."

The colonel was right. The peace treaty had been broken by Iran. They had broken yet another peace plan that was to them nothing more than a meaningless excuse to buy time and then ignore when it suited their purposes. The colonel was also right about the devastation that was to come, which would prove to be far greater than the 32 planes that fell from the sky and crashed that night.

The minutes went by, and then hours. News crews in the affected region had no equipment that would work and therefore they could not broadcast the news. The governments of the affected countries weren't saying much to shed light on what had happened anyway.

When dawn broke the next morning, the world still had little idea of what had happened, but that began to change with the new day. Helicopters began to fly into the region. They saw cities at a stand still. They found some of the aircraft crash sites. Reporters were on some of the helicopters that landed in Kuwait and other places. They made broadcasts to report what had happened the night before and relate the current situation.

Steve had not returned home yet from his all-night shift at work. Mary awoke early that morning and turned the TV on while preparing to depart for work. She began to hear about the big news that had happened overnight.

Steve then walked in the front door. "Steve," Mary almost shouted, "Have you heard about what happened?"

Steve almost laughed on the inside. "Yes," he replied. "I had a rather eventful night at the office."

They sat down and compared notes. Steve did most of the talking as Mary sat in near disbelief over what she was hearing. Then Steve said, "Be careful when you get to work. There may be reporters and press conferences. Find out what information they want released, and stick to that and nothing more. I may have told you more than I should have."

Citizens and governments began to ask for assistance. Little did they realize that things had only just begun to deteriorate since it was summertime; summertime in the desert. As the day wore on, the temperature hit 115 degrees. There was no air conditioning—even simple electrical fans would not work. Water pumping stations use electrical pumps. Now these wouldn't work and the flow of water stopped. There was no water for bathing. The only drinking water was a very short supply of bottled drinking water. Refrigerators, like everything else electrical, were rendered useless. All perishable food started to rot. At 115 degrees, that happens very quickly. Rotting food also becomes a major health hazard quickly. Rescue workers and recovery crews were unable to get to many of the aircraft crash sites, and some crash sites had not even yet been found.

Communications also ground to a halt. Phones did not work. The TV broadcasts that were now being done only by foreign crews with equipment they had brought with them were able to utilize their normal communication satellites and broadcast worldwide, but couldn't broadcast to that region because it takes both power and TVs that are working and not zapped in order to receive and watch the broadcasts. This part of the world now had neither.

In Kuwait, the smallest of the four countries and the closest to the blast, the impact was greatest since the shutdown affected that entire country. The inhabitants were not getting answers. They wanted information, assistance and services, but they were getting nothing. They quickly started to panic. Security systems were not working, other than doors, locks, guard dogs and fences. Riots and looting began in some areas, and people were going after far more than just bottled water.

As Steve continued to watch TV news coverage, the scene now shifted to America where the first reports came of the nuclear disaster that had occurred in New York City.

The survivors there wished they only had to deal with no power, no transportation, no phones and no drinking water on a hot day. The problems there were much more severe than that. They had lost much of their rescue force, hospitals, communications and all infrastructure, and also had to fear the still-present radiation. New York was fairly well-prepared for a more conventional strike, such as the bombing of a building or bridge or aircraft. However, they now had to deal with something much larger that they were not prepared for; that no city or nation could be prepared for.

In the aftermath of 9–11 years ago, people watched extensive news coverage of the gripping scenes and clean-up. This time around, however, things were so much worse that people just couldn't handle the news. The nation was in shock and didn't know what to do or how to proceed.

As the days went by in Kuwait and the Middle East, the continuance of life itself became the top priority of everyone. People can live without water for only about four days. What limited food and water that existed was used by people at the expense of livestock, which started to die from heat and lack of water. Disease began to break out due to this. That caused further panic.

As though conditions weren't already bad enough, the damage so far had been limited to this area, a circle of about 260 miles in diameter covering Kuwait and smaller portions of three other countries. However, this was about to change drastically. All four of these nations in this part of the world were major oil producers. Oil fields and the drilling and pumping of oil from beneath the surface to pipelines, refineries and ships are all controlled by a huge network of electric pumps, relays and sensors. All such operations came to a complete standstill when the EMP occurred. What's more, even in the unaffected parts of Saudi Arabia, Iraq and Iran to the west, north and east that still had power and could pump oil could not send the oil toward Kuwait in the network of pipelines to get the oil onto tanker ships in the Persian Gulf for worldwide sales and distribution. That network of pipelines is controlled electronically and was now inoperative. Nothing could be done manually to get it working. Nothing, that is, short of replacing every electronic component in the system, but that would take months.

The world quickly started to feel the huge impact of this. Approximately 55% of the world's oil supply flows through the Persian Gulf from these four countries. That huge supply of oil had now dried up completely and stopped.

The world's commodity traders started to do what they do best—they overreacted and panicked in a state of fear and greed and wildly bid up the price of oil, breaking the $150 level, but it was nowhere near done. Breaching the $150 barrier made people fear the end was not in sight, and they were right. In the weeks ahead, oil jumped to $160, then $170 and before long it hit $175. At that point, it took a breather and settled back down to $165 where it seemed to establish a new base.

Back in the U.S., away from the New York City area, people struggled to go on with their lives. Gasoline hit $6 a gallon. This had a widespread impact. People cut back on their driving, especially discretionary driving like vacations. The airline and trucking industries got hit hard by higher costs and had to cut back on services and increase prices. The price of products made from oil like tires and plastics went way up. The inflation rate jumped to 18% annualized, a number never before seen in the country. Interest rates had no alternative but to skyrocket along with the inflation rate.

New York City is the nation's financial center due to Wall Street and many bank headquarters being there, but all that was out of commission. Trading was transferred to make-shift trading floors in Chicago, the center of commodities trading. It was questionable if things would run smoothly even if trading was in a normal pattern, but these were not normal times.

The run-up in inflation and interest rates meant that the bond market would plummet, and it did. The public came to realize the negative impact of this since the bond market is even larger than the stock market. Consumer confidence took a nosedive. The stock markets did some nose diving of their own. The currency markets, larger than the bond or stock market, also suffered severe gyrations, due to both the New York situation and the world situation as a whole.

Similar economic and financial disasters happened in all the developed nations of the world. Before long, gasoline at any price became hard to find in many places. Some people simply could not afford it, while in some parts of the U.S. and overseas it was just not available or was in limited supply. In many cities, people suffered through long lines at gas stations.

Farmers were also hit hard by the spike in gas costs. Many could not afford to run their tractors and other machinery and went out of business. Before long, this led to a famine. A famine is normally when a lack of rain decreases crop production, but in this case a different problem led to the same result. Grocery store shelves started to be depleted. This didn't happen overnight and was worse in some places than others, but between a decreasing crop supply and a decreasing number of truckers delivering goods, grocery shortages started to occur in many cities.

The U.S. and the rest of the world had already been in the midst of a depression. Getting hit quickly by all these additional forces caused an inflationary depression and things became even worse. Businesses were going under, tax revenue was hurting, unemployment was increasing, and on top of the many economic hardships, disease and starvation were running rampant in many parts of the world and people were dying.

The world was desperately looking for leadership. In America, the media had helped get the president it wanted elected a couple of years ago in the 2008 election; a president that stood for little except higher taxes and wanting America to mind its own business, and somehow got elected anyway. This played right into the hands of the globalism agenda of the radical Council on Foreign Relations and the Trilateral Commission. They got what they wanted, but the times now called for extraordinary leadership and courage. However, it was becoming clear that the president was not up to such a challenge. In fact, the president might have been as bad as Jimmy Carter had been.

Former President Carter had been in the news recently due to his death. His legacy extended from his botched handling of the 1979 Iranian hostage crisis and the economic malaise he left behind when he left office, to his 2006 book called *Palestine: Peace not Apartheid,* where just a quick glance at the jacket cover made it clear he still couldn't see the obvious. It was Carter who engineered the fall of the Shah of Iran that led to Iran becoming the danger it had been for years. He incorrectly blamed Israel for decades of hostilities in the Middle East, thereby contributing to the problems there. Until Carter's last day, he acted like it was Israel who took dozens of Americans hostage and humiliated him for over a year. When his life was reviewed as it always is in death, everyone looking objectively could plainly see that he may have been the worst American president ever.

Carter may have been the worst, that is, until now. The current president seemed to be challenging him for that title. With poor policies, lack of policies and indecision, the president had helped to end America's dominance as a world leader, although that was a long process that had gone on for years with the help of an ineffective Congress. Now the challenges were even bigger. When the world needed leadership most as it did now, America had little to offer. China had spent years growing into a world economic power but never developed the kind of government that could handle a worldwide crisis. Russia had regained much of its old strength, but like America and China, it also did not have any Churchills, Roosevelts or Reagans to offer. Should Roosevelt even be on such a list? It was his New Deal that started the government explosion in bureaucracy and overspending as it began to baby-sit people with welfare, social security, and much more to come.

Every country, in fact the entire world, wanted someone to step into the role of decisive leader and fix the world's many, serious problems. There was one man though who seemed ready for the extraordinary challenge. Ricardo Valentine still served as Secretary General of the United Nations. He had spent the last few years working with world leaders to address some of the growing challenges. The problems had grown way beyond what could be fixed by the actions of any one nation. Worldwide changes were needed to avert further worsening of the problems. Valentine had been in Europe lately pursuing this globalism further which had kept him safe from the New York attack.

Valentine planned an increased role for the UN and himself. He decided the time was right to present his plan to the world, and that he would do it from the sight of his greatest triumph—the recently finished temple in Jerusalem that his Middle East peace plan had laid the ground work for.

The peace plan had been broken by Iran's attempted attack, following the example of Yasser Arafat, who was by no means the first Arab leader to use this deceitful tactic of signing a treaty and then ignoring it. Islamic leaders had done the same thing time and time again for 1,400 years. And why not? Their very own Quran not only condones violence, but commands it. This led to centuries of violence and bloodshed in the name of a god that a man made up. That founder was assassinated, as were three of his next four successors; quite a reflection of their tactics and mindset.

The Quran orders that if pagans resist Islam, they must fight and slay them wherever they are found; lie in wait for them, seize them, and beleaguer them. The punishment for those who oppose them is exile, cutting off limbs, or death. In fact, any Muslim who rejects these tenets of their religion is to be killed himself.

Some Islamic leaders have stated that they intend to take over the land of the Vatican and humiliate its occupants or convert them to Islam. This is despite the fact that decades before, the pope agreed with them and fought against the reestablishment of Israel in 1948, since he and his church were strongly opposed to such a thing. More recently, Pope John Paul II did not support Israel, did not think Jews could go to heaven despite being God's chosen people, and publicly bowed to and kissed a Quran. Still, Muslims cannot find peace with anyone no matter how much someone seeks peace by groveling, appeasing, defying God and vilifying God's chosen nation Israel.

Once again though, the world ignored all this and did not condemn Iran for their hostile and unprovoked launch of a nuclear missile at Israel, but instead, blamed Israel for their defensive reaction that led to the EMP and the resulting worldwide oil shortage and devastation.

In order to attempt to improve the image of Israel and seek the return to peace that Israel sought, Valentine reasoned that it was appropriate to make his address from the temple. The temple had been completed just six months ago after a three year period of construction. It was one of only a very few events the world could rally behind in these recent, troubled times. The temple represented both history and the future, defeat and triumph, unity and hope. It was a building of 180 feet in height whose meaning and magnificence said much about the human spirit. What better place to go forth with a message that could potentially change and rally the world.

Two weeks after beginning the preparation for this historic address by Mr. Valentine, everything was ready. Mr. Valentine was in his seat in the Great Hall of the temple in front of TV cameras and gave the following address to a worldwide audience in English, translated into many languages:

> "The world has suffered many traumas in recent history. We've seen devastation from earthquakes, droughts, famines, disease, shortages of oil and other resources, a depression, wars that still rage on today, a return to a nuclear age, and the on-going threat that such devices may be used again. We are facing both economic and geopolitical problems. There seems to be nothing for citizens to put their faith in. There's no escaping the fact that people are hurting and scared. There's no

escaping the fact that things will continue to get worse unless we implement changes to find a different path.

"Technology has made the world smaller. Business, trade and the economy have become global. The depression we are now suffering through was caused by the out-of-date old-world economic tools and systems that were kept in place well beyond their useful life.

"Therefore, I now propose for your consideration a different path; a path for escape. This path has to include major reforms in the way we conduct business because nothing less than major changes will work to modernize the world and return us to safety and prosperity. For several years now the continents have been merging their governments, trade, banking and currencies. It has worked well with the European Union, as one example.

"I propose as Step #1 that we now take this concept a step further and merge these multiple governing bodies into a single world government. Such a governing body would be better able to provide oversight of international legislation, banking, travel and immigration, health, emergency management, and commerce. Such a body could steer our escape from the depression by implementing changes on a worldwide basis, not just in a single country.

"To further expedite this process, I propose as Step #2 a single worldwide currency. The European Union's success with the Euro shows the value and wisdom of such a step. A currency managed by a Central World Bank will fix the nightmarish problems we are facing today by letting us start over with a managed currency that will work. How will we do this? I use the term "currency" only figuratively. There would not actually be paper money that we are used to. It would be replaced by electronic banking cards less prone to theft and counterfeiting than currencies. More importantly, a single currency system would end inflation and deflation since the value of the currency would not go up or down versus other currencies, since other currencies would no longer exist. Currency speculating has never contributed anything to productivity, manufacturing or providing services. Moving to a single currency and a cashless society will end the wild currency fluctuations that contributed greatly to the financial market chaos we've all seen. This would fix our economic woes. This would enable us to escape the clutches of what has dragged down the nations of the world."

Mr. Valentine continued on for twenty more minutes explaining how he had been in touch with world leaders who were generally in agreement with implementing such a system. He also added some detail outlining specific steps proposed to make all this possible and to do it quickly. He offered reassurance to a worldwide audience of people who generally do not like change in their lives.

The world had never experienced a speech quite like this. The ability to do a live, worldwide broadcast had existed for years, and was in fact used routinely for major events like the Super Bowl, Princess Diana's funeral and scenes from 9–11, but no one could recall a person addressing a world-wide audience in quite this manner.

Additionally, the importance of the speech was enormous. The speech had in fact been reassuring and seemed to offer worthwhile ideas and hope for a better tomorrow. People wondered far and wide what the world's reaction would be and if it could work.

Exodus to the Promised Land

The Van de Kamp family had intently watched the speech at their home in nearby Tel Aviv. It didn't take them or anyone long to get a feel for the world's reaction to what quickly became known as the "Escape from the Abyss" speech. The reaction was very positive. People were desperate and ready and willing to try anything that seemed to have a chance of working and leading to reform, especially if it seemed to come from a strong leader. A worldwide grass roots groundswell of change was quickly in the air.

Steve and Mary came to that conclusion after watching news reports much of that day. Later in the day, Mary asked Steve, "Do you see what's coming?"

Steve looked at her and said, "Yes. You were right. It's happening."

Jeff asked them both, "What's happening?"

"The Tribulation is happening," Mary answered. "Just like I've been saying, all these disasters happening around the world are not just random occurrences. Some people have known that times such as these were coming, but didn't know when. Now we know when because they're happening right before our eyes."

"What about this new plan by Valentine and the UN?" Jeff asked. "Maybe this will lead to Israel's return to prominence that people keep mentioning. Maybe the world government and bank will be headquartered right here."

"Maybe," Steve said, "but it won't work. The UN is as corrupt as ever, and Valentine is no savior. He's just the opposite. As convincing as his speech sounded, he doesn't have the well-being of anybody in mind but himself. He's going to become a world leader and lead the world right into its demise."

"What should we do?" a concerned Mary asked.

"It's time to go," Steve said. "Just like we've talked about, it's time to put our future in the hands of God and leave here. I know it sounds scary, but we have to trust what we know and trust what we've been told. Doing so has always worked before, and it won't be just us anyway. We won't be alone." Steve thought, and then he added, "Mary, tomorrow when you go to work, you should make the broadcast we've talked about."

"Okay, but it's scary," she said.

Steve needed to reassure her. He felt fortunate that he was pretty good at knowing when and how to do so as he began, "Mary, I don't ever look at you without thinking I'm the luckiest guy on earth for meeting you. It's a miracle the way me met, not once but twice. We've been right where we're supposed to be in this world, and we've fulfilled God's plan for us so far, but that plan is not through. He has an important job for you tomorrow. You're the right person to do this. You're the best communicator I know, and you'll be great. Do this big job, and then afterwards we'll leave here and see what's next."

The next day, Mary went to the U.S. Embassy where she had worked for the last few years. Due to the strong relationship the U.S. and Israel had shared for many years, the U.S. Embassy in Tel Aviv was very large and had become a communications center of sorts. Mary worked as both a Public Affairs Officer and Communications Officer, two related fields. That day, Mary made a radio broadcast to address the nation with what amounted to a short but important public service announcement. She said the following:

> "To my adopted homeland, the nation of Israel, my name is Mary Van de Kamp, coming to you with a vital message. Yesterday's worldwide address by the UN Secretary General might seem like an attractive path forward that the world seems to be buying into, but there are those who know otherwise. In the last three and a half years, half of the world's population has died. What we heard proposed yesterday is a deceitful, temporary fix. The two witnesses who have been speaking at the temple have warned us to run from this.

> "Throughout its existence, Israel experienced a hardening and has been blinded to the identity of the true deliverer who will come from Zion and turn godlessness away from this great nation. It is time for those of us who believe and understand this to flee from here and from the false deliverer before things get worse. Some of you know what I speak of.

"God has made a special provision for those of us who heed his call; a place prepared for us in the desert where we will be taken care of and protected from the considerable wrath that is to come. For those of you who wish to be protected and in His presence, please join us at noon two days from now at the Jewish Quarter of the Old City in Jerusalem, where we will seek His face, and seek this place."

Mary had delivered her impassioned plea beautifully. She then went to see her supervisor and resigned. Steve likewise had resigned that day from his job. They each had long and illustrious careers, had been well paid, and had no doubts about the appropriateness of the action they were taking.

They met at home that night and hugged. Steve had heard Mary's radio address and was proud of her. It was time for them to do some packing in preparation for leaving in two days for good, and to also see neighbors to encourage them to come, and say good-bye if they wouldn't. Steve felt a little like one of the apostles who had suddenly been selected by Jesus to leave behind the life he knew to follow him. It was a very strange but good feeling.

The one who wasn't totally on-board with this was Jeff. He was now a young adult who was still living with Steve and Mary and had been attending college for three years and was doing quite well. He was nearing graduation and the start of a promising career, and it seemed hard to give it up and leave for the great unknown. He talked to his dad that night about it.

"Dad, it's like you're going on a weird spring break trip; a caravan ride through the desert. Aren't you just going to run out of gas and be back soon? Shouldn't I just stay here?"

"I can't make you come," Steve said, "but have you forgotten the readings from your 11th grade Bible as Literature class? You've seen the Bible prophecies coming true all around us. Don't you remember what's next?"

Jeff shook his head no.

Steve had the information on the tip of his tongue. "The final seven plagues of God's wrath are coming next. People are going to be covered with horribly painful sores. The water in the oceans will turn to blood, and then all the inland sources of fresh water will turn to blood. The sun will scorch people with heat and fire and part of the earth will get burned up, and then the world will be thrown into darkness. People will be tortured for five months. Many people will die. Finally, the Euphrates River will dry up and allow a huge army to gather, and then the army will invade this country for the battle at Armageddon. You don't want to be here."

Jeff asked, "Why is God taking out his wrath on us?"

Steve knew that was a natural question that deserved a good reply. "Like it says in 2 Peter 3:9, God does not want anybody to perish, so He has patiently waited and gave the world many prophets and prophesies that came true, and now recently gave us the two witnesses. He gave us signs through people, nature and circumstances. He gave us miracles. He gave us the Bible. He gave us the church. He gave us warnings. He gave us intelligence to see the warnings. What more is He supposed to do—come down here in person and warn us some more? He already did that too. His name was Jesus, and we killed him. His judgment of the world is fair and its time has come, just like He foretold us. If all that's not enough though and you're still not sure, think about it and decide tomorrow."

The next day didn't take long to provide news to further guide Jeff and all people. The two witnesses mentioned recently by both Mary and Steve had been killed overnight. These two witnesses had mysteriously appeared a few years ago and had been prophesying in and around Jerusalem, the eternal holy city, ever since. Now they had been suddenly murdered, and no one knew how it happened.

When Jeff heard this, he said to Steve and Mary, "You were right. How did you know that would happen?"

Mary replied, "God told us in the Bible. It's right there for people to read, along with some detail about what's ahead."

"Alright, I'm going with you," Jeff said, relieved that his decision now seemed completely clear and easy.

"Good," his dad said. "You'll see that this will have eternal value. That's what we should pursue everyday."

The next day, the three of them finished preparations and left by car for Jerusalem for the rendezvous, not really knowing what they would find or what lay ahead. When they reached Jerusalem, they realized that the city seemed more unique and important every time they saw it.

What they found when they arrived was a large crowd that had been growing all morning long in and around the Old City. The crowd was wondering, like Steve and Mary, who was in charge and what it was they were going to do. Due to the on-going gas shortage, some people had given up their cars and arrived by foot. It seemed to Steve and Mary and everyone else that this was going to become some sort of slow-paced caravan that would head off into the desert in some direction, just like Jeff said.

Shortly after noon, a rabbi led a large group of the gatherers in prayer and asked for God's direction. Their prayer seemed to be answered when a cloud appeared on top of the Old City's wall. "Look!" the rabbi exclaimed. "That's our sign. We are to follow the cloud where it leads us."

With that, the large, slow group set out to do just that and followed the cloud as it moved before them to the south out of town. Some of those on foot had found someone to ride with, but some proceeded on foot so the whole procession went at that pace. It was quite a strange site.

As day turned to night after a beautiful sunset, the cloud continued and glowed as though lit by a fire. Eight miles outside of town, the group stopped to spend the night. People slept in cars and on the ground in an area they turned into a large makeshift campground. Steve had brought sleeping bags for his family in case such a thing happened. He estimated the crowd to be about 5,000 people in size.

The next morning, the group continued onward. As they headed into the more sparsely populated southeastern parts of the country, some vehicles ran out of gas. Those occupants calmly loaded their goods into the vehicles of those willing to help and continued on. SUVs that could handle any terrain, especially those with auxiliary fuel tanks that owners had topped off, became valuable commodities.

As they slowly moved along, Jeff asked Steve to tell him more of what he knew about Armageddon.

Steve told him what he could think of. "The world will continue to blame its suffering from the EMP on Israel, and soon the plagues I told you about will occur. Satan will surely get everyone to blame Israel for them too. To prevent more plagues, to get revenge and to finally annihilate their enemy, an army of the world will be raised and united and come to do battle against Israel. The false deliverer will unite the armies of all the nations and advance them to Armageddon, intent on wiping out everybody in this country.

Jeff wondered something and said, "Not every nation. The U.S. won't join and fight against its ally."

"Maybe not, but the U.S. will at least not try to stop any of this, and that's just as bad. God will crumble America's empire, just like he's done to every empire that opposed His people.

"What do you mean?" Jeff asked.

Steve replied, "You've heard of the Great British Empire, the Empire so big the sun never set on it. That tiny country basically ruled the world for 200 years not that long ago, but met their demise when they betrayed the Jews. After World War I, a big tract of land was destined to become the Jewish National Home, but in 1922 Britain gave over 3/4ths of it away to the Arabs for what became Jordan because Britain felt an Arab alliance was to their advantage. Then the British army captured many Jews and sent them to Europe where Hitler killed them in the Holocaust. In 1948, Britain had a lot to do with the UN giving Israel as little land as it did."

What about the U.S.?" Jeff asked. What did we do wrong?"

"We got as stupid as Britain did. Bush's Roadmap for Peace was a roadmap for disaster. Bush gave away God's land. It started in 2002, and eventually we caused Israel to give away Gaza in 2005. Hezbollah and al-Qaeda both moved in there and we did nothing to stop them. Then we had them give away the West Bank, and then we wanted Israel to give away a big portion of Jerusalem, to be used as a Palestinian capital of all things. Before that, the Clinton administration gave hundreds of millions of dollars to Arafat's PLO, and did nothing when Arafat used the money to support his terrorist network. The U.S. Department of State has hated Israel since Day 1 in 1948. And to top it off, there's this giant double standard where the U.S. says they will not negotiate with terrorists, but expects Israel to do just that."

Steve continued, "The Bible warns of God's judgment

upon those who meddle in the Middle East and defy what God decreed for his people like we've done. For example, in Genesis 12:3, God says He will bless those who bless Israel and curse those who curse Israel. He's been true to His word. In Joel 3:2, God says He will gather all nations and enter judgment against them concerning those who divided up the land of His people Israel. Jeremiah 12:14 says that wicked neighbors who seize the inheritance God gave Israel will be uprooted from their lands and destroyed. That's what the U.S. and all nations did and that's why the U.S. has been suffering like every other nation, and it will be no different at Armageddon."

"Tell me about the battle at Armageddon," Jeff asked. "What will happen?"

"First, heaven will open and Jesus will return to earth, followed by the armies of heaven all riding on horses. It will be Jesus and this army of His church against the armies of the world which will probably be led by Russia and the Arab states. They will assemble in the Valley of Armageddon north of Jerusalem, intent upon advancing to Jerusalem to attack, but that will never happen. As fierce and unbeatable as an army of the world sounds, they will be on the losing side. There will be a lot of build up, but then not much of a battle. The army of Christ won't need to wield swords or shoot guns or anything. Christ will defeat the huge enemy army with nothing more than speaking some words with the sword of his mouth."

"That's it?" Jeff asked. "Then they fall down dead or what?"

"Actually," Steve said, "there will be more than that. After the words of Jesus, there will be great flashes of lightning and deafening thunder. The enemy will be seized with panic and attack each other. Their skin, eyes and tongues will rot. Huge hailstones of about 100 pounds each will fall on the army. The largest hailstone ever recorded only weighed two pounds; these will be 100 pounds. It couldn't be more appropriate."

"What do you mean?" Jeff asked.

"That's God's imagination and justice at work again. God judges us the way we judge others. He also let's the punishment fit the crime. He's done so over and over. Think of it. Pharaoh drowned the Hebrew babies in the Nile River, so God killed all first-born Egyptians at Passover, and then God drowned Pharaoh and his army in the Red Sea after Moses led his people through. Pharaoh had chosen the form of death that would be used against him. Now 3,500 years later, the enemy tried to rain down chaos and terror on us from the sky above with their EMP, so that's exactly how God will deal with them in retaliation. His lightning and hail from above will destroy their army."

Steve continued, "Then there will be a huge earthquake, an earthquake such as the world has never experienced before that will be felt worldwide. It will cause destruction in cities and nations everywhere on earth and even affect countries that may not participate in the army. God will then have fulfilled what it says in Ezekiel 38:23–'I will make myself known in the sight of many nations. Then they will know that I am the Lord.'"

The next day, the caravan was moving along at its regular slow pace. Mary found a station on the car's radio. The family heard a news story about how there had been a bad earthquake back in Jerusalem during the night. It was feared that several thousand lives had been lost along with there being much damage and a general state of panic.

"Just like we expected," Mary said. "The final death toll

will come to 7,000 people who could have been here and been saved but chose to stay behind, exactly like we read."

That gave everybody something to think about as they proceeded along that day. Jeff also thought about how his plans had changed. He had planned on finishing up college soon and thought his next big decision would be whether to return to the U.S. or not. His plans had changed!

Mary thought about her life and how it emulated that of Esther from the Old Testament. Esther lived through some strange circumstances which eventually resulted in the deliverance of God's people, which Mary also did.

Then there was Steve, who thought about how his life paralleled Job's, a man also from the Old Testament. Job had it all, then lost it all, but he trusted God and ultimately got it all back and more. Steve felt like he had gotten it all back with Mary alone, but also had so much more than that.

As the sun started to go down later that day, Steve knew that Mary always got a little uneasy when darkness started to fall. He even felt the same way himself, so he said to her, "Try not to worry. When we worry, we're just usurping God's job. He even says, 'For who by worrying can add a day to his life?'" Then Steve started to sing to her a song that had always been a favorite of theirs:

> If a man could be two places at one time,
> I'd be with you.
> Tomorrow and today, beside you all the way.
> If the world should stop revolving spinning
> slowly down to die,
> I'd spend the end with you.
> And when the world was through,
> Then one by one the stars would all go out,
> Then you and I would simply fly away.

That's what they had been doing for a few days now: flying away to a place in the desert prepared ahead of time for their safety and protection as it says in Revelation 12:14.

Ahead of them, the vehicles were suddenly all coming to a stand still. The cloud that had led the group was still there, and was leading them into a canyon. It was decided the group would spend the night at that spot, and decide how to proceed in the morning.

The next morning, the cloud still shone in the same spot. The leaders all agreed to proceed into the canyon ahead. This took a leap of faith, since the canyon could not be traversed by vehicles and it meant everyone would have to abandon the vehicles and proceed on foot. Everyone proceeded rather joyously, thinking this meant their journey was probably near its end.

The group walked through a long, narrow gorge that cut through a mountainside. The gorge was only about 20 to 30 feet across and over 100 feet deep. After a mile or so, the gorge got so deep and dark that it seemed like a dead end must be ahead. Instead though, they suddenly emerged into a sun-lit valley. The mountain basin was full of what looked like old temples and tombs cut into the sides of the cliffs that formed the valley walls.

Steve, Mary and Jeff were together and looked upon the site in awe. As they walked along, they saw an amazing, two-story tall façade that had been carved into the canyon wall.

Jeff said, "I recognize that. I've seen it before somewhere."

Mary said, "Me too. We're in Petra. The ancient city of Petra. I've heard of this place and always wanted to visit here. Who knew we'd wind up here under these circumstances?"

Steve said, "Yes, it makes perfect sense. In the book of Daniel, it says the land of Edom will be saved from the invaders. Petra was the capital of Edom. Plus Petra means rock, and Isaiah 2:10 says to enter into the rocks and hide."

The Van de Kamps and 5,000 others were indeed getting their first glimpse of their new home, Petra. The city had been carved out of these cliffs starting about 300 BC and grew into a city of trade. That lasted for centuries until an earthquake led to its obscurity around 500 AD. It was rediscovered well over a thousand years later. Today, it sits as a magnificent mountain fortress protected by its very limited access—the narrow gorge the group had just traversed. With those thoughts in mind, the family walked around and took in the sites.

With its remoteness, inaccessibility, and plentiful water supply, Petra was the spot where this relatively small handful of people would spend the next three and one half years isolated and supernaturally protected from the world during the second half of the Tribulation, the Great Tribulation. The rest of the world would continue to suffer the wrath of God as He gave people one final chance to repent, and cleansed the earth with the seven plagues in preparation for the return of His Son and the reclamation and reward of His few believers, for this is the destiny in the story of mankind.

WRITER'S NOTE - WHAT'S NEXT?

Here the story ends...for now. In the future, the nation of Israel will in fact by invaded by an army of millions intent upon finally destroying it. Smaller armies have already attempted to do so several times since Israel became a nation again on May 14, 1948. The very next day they were attacked by the coalition forces of five neighboring nations, but somehow Israel's small army triumphed. The same thing has unfolded multiple times since then, and the work of God has been in evidence many times to save the nation.

In 2003, American forces were heading north through southern Iraq toward Baghdad trying to unseat Saddam Hussein. There was a large windstorm for about 24 hours that brought all movement to a halt. The war was so much in the news those days that you may recall this. Much less reported than this storm though was the fact that after the storm, thousands of landmines that had been buried were now exposed since the wind had blown the dirt and sand away. This saved countless lives of American soldiers.

Israeli military officers have many similar stories to tell about battles fought in their country that they won despite overwhelming odds against them. These are called miracles.

We are surrounded by them everyday; we just don't really notice them and in fact, we take them for granted if and when we notice them at all. These are the miracles of a sunrise or sunset, rainbows, waterfalls, ocean waves, birds singing, flowers blooming, the birth of a baby, and so much more. We chalk all this up to Mother Nature and give God no credit, but there are no laws of nature; there are only the laws of God which nature complies with. This is one of our many mistakes, and an example of how we keep moving further and further away from God.

Back to this novel, and its implications for the human race. Many of the events described in this book have actually happened or are happening today. Many of the extraordinary events in the future as described in the second half of this book will happen. We have been told so in Daniel chapters 9–12, Ezekiel chapters 38–39, Jeremiah chapters 50–52, Joel chapters 2–3, Jude, Matthew chapter 24, Zechariah chapters 12–14, and especially the book of Revelation.

I don't know exactly how events will unfold leading up to this novel's final chapter, but some scenario will occur leading up to what looks like the inevitable destruction of God's chosen people and chosen nation of Israel. We do not need to fear the outcome though for them or for ourselves because we can know the outcome—it has been told to us. Divine intervention will occur, this time on a massive scale. No human author has enough foresight or imagination to conceive of exactly how it will happen, but it will start with words from the mouth of the Son of Man Himself when he has returned to earth. No one knows if it will take seconds, minutes, hours or days, but there will be a huge storm and massive earthquake that will flatten mountains and make islands disappear, and possibly some other event that gets the enemy army to panic and destroy itself. We know the outcome, and we know that believers will have nothing to worry about.

How can anybody know the events and the outcome? Quite simply because God told us so. God wrote a long letter to us that we should all read. We've all heard of it—it's the Bible. It is the inspired word of God Himself (2 Timothy 3:16). The events of the novel's final chapter are clearly described in the Bible. Unfortunately, those who study such things tell us that only a very small fraction of us ever read it; about 2%. We spend about ten years of our lives working at a job to earn money that all gets spent, eight years watching TV, six years eating, and even spend five years reading, but we never read the one book written by the Creator, the one book that matters, the one book that contains truth, the one book that is the source of wisdom and knowledge. The Bible's last Book, the Book of Revelation, even contains the following statement:

> "Blessed is the one who reads the words of this prophecy, and blessed are those who hear it and take to heart what is written in it, because the time is near." *(Revelation 1:3)*

Please do as God encourages us to do and join the 2% who have read the Bible; read it and believe it and let it be your source of truth. In Matthew 7:23, Jesus says, "I never knew you. Away from me." I doubt that anyone can know Jesus and go to heaven without reading His word. Far more important than my opinion though is what Jesus said in Mark 8:38:

"If anyone is ashamed of me and my words, the Son of Man will be ashamed of him when he comes in his Father's glory."

There are hundreds of religions in the world. They are not different means of arriving at the same place. At most, just one of them is correct and valid; everyone else is following a false religion and therefore not really worshipping God. If you've never read the bible, how do you know that you've made the right choice? What are the odds you made the right choice? People in all but one religion are following a false, man-made doctrine. Even if your religion has millions of followers, there's no safety or validity in that.

Don't be put off by those who claim the Bible is too difficult, out-of-touch, or out-of-date. Don't tell yourself you have better things to do; things that matter more. If you could ask God if going to church or reading the Bible is more important, I think he'd say reading the Bible. Think about it—what's more important: hearing what men have to say that may or may not be accurate, or reading what God has to tell us that you know you can depend on? Don't get me wrong—the Bible says go to church—but reading God's word should come first and foremost as your basis for everything and as the source of your wisdom and knowledge.

Everybody has heard the story of how Moses led the Israelite slaves out of Egypt. Read the equally incredible story in Genesis about how they got there in the first place. Read about the life of Jesus. After Jesus, the world's next most important person was probably the Apostle Paul. Read what he has to say. Read about the start of Christianity and its basis. Read about what will happen in the Book of Revelation.

The United States has many problems. Some are being addressed well, some are being addressed poorly, and many are not being addressed at all. I'd like to see the U.S. Government return to its roots. However, communicating the message of God was my primary purpose in writing this book. Did you notice in Chapter 14 where it stated that half the world's population died? This is not fiction. That will happen. In fact, it will be more than half. It will not be pretty and it will not be painless. There will be widespread suffering. It may easily happen during our lifetimes, or the lifetimes of our children. Many enormous events will cause this: multiple severe earthquakes, disease, famine, the sun being darkened, fresh water becoming undrinkable, and much more. It will be like the 10 plagues on Pharaoh and Egypt, but on a much larger scale. This is the price to be paid for man's long history of trying to bend, break and force into submission the will of others through any means including war. There may also be the detonation of nuclear bombs in this process. This is God's process for cleaning up the earth before the return of His Son, the second coming, an event we are all exhorted to seek and long for (2 Timothy 4:8). Why does the earth need cleaning up? Our only enemy should be Satan, but the history of mankind is one of endless wars with each other instead.

The Bible also describes what is called the Rapture. Many people don't believe this will happen. They apparently do not believe what God told us in 1 Thessalonians 4:16. Many don't think anyone will be taken away in the Rapture. Among other things, the Rapture interferes with the false man-made concept of purgatory, which many people prefer to believe. Those with the wisdom to have read and believe the Bible's clear statements know the Rapture will happen, although no one knows exactly how or when it will happen. In one of the many mysteries that God left unanswered for us, we don't know for sure when it will happen in relation to these other events. Believers will probably be taken away before the misery and suffering of the Tribulation, but that's not a given.

It's been said by some believers that they wouldn't want a God they could fully understand and comprehend. I find this to be a meaningful and accurate saying. Can any of us really conceive of the process of building massive planets and the sun and the rest of the universe? Centuries ago, wouldn't we all have thought the earth was the center of the universe and that the sun revolved around us, as an example of how limited our mind is? God came up with a universe that far exceeds the imagination that any of us have. He still knows things we can't conceive of. He can do things we can't conceive of.

A popular saying nowadays is, "I'm not religious; I'm spiritual." That sounds good and could be taken in a good way. It could mean that someone thinks "religion" is just a works-based process invented by man that consists of traditions and ceremonies that may or may not really glorify God (and they'd be right), whereas being "spiritual" is the process of really getting to know and glorify God without all the trappings of the man-made part. That sounds good, but this often is not the case. "Spirituality" these days more often than not is a feel-good term used by many man-made religions and movements that basically encompass a feel-good message to do and believe whatever makes you feel good. However, in the eyes of God, this has all the actual value of the many commercials these days that end with the words, "because you deserve it!"

What we all deserve is eternity in hell because we are all sinners. That is not exactly a "feel good" statement, but God says it is so (Romans 3:23). We should certainly know this and believe it. Anyone who thinks or hopes they are good enough to overcome their sins by virtue of their works or religion is badly uninformed, misled, or in denial (John 14:6, Galatians 2:21). Anyone who thinks they are living their best life now is paying attention to the massive American marketing machine, but unfortunately not the word of God. They are not thinking in terms of heaven or eternity, or saving up for themselves treasures in heaven.

Christ died on the cross for us, for our sins, and in place of us so that hell did not have to be our destiny. When Jesus prayed the night before His death and sweated blood, it was not the thought of the pain that He feared; it's that He hated the thought of turning from the Father by taking on our sins—that's what He did! We shouldn't waste His death, what we put Him through, or our chance at a glorious future in heaven which God (the Father, Son and Holy Spirit) wants us to enjoy. In heaven, we can continue to live out the chief aim of man like we should be now, which is:

To know God and glorify and enjoy Him forever.